The Moon Can Tell

July 2018
For Signe — my favorite
young horseman at the
AERC endurance rides! Keep
it up! Love for horses forever ♡
love Dana

A NOVEL

Dana S. Frank

BY

Dana Frank

Dana Frank is a writer who lives in the wilds west of Austin, Texas, where she and her husband raised their son and daughter and now make do with four horses, two cats, and a dog.

Text is set in Untitled Serif.

Back cover: The author with her parents by the American hospital in Munich, Germany. Photo by Lisa Landry, née Moring.

Front cover photo by Julie Savasky.

Book and cover design by
Julie Savasky, Austin, Texas.

To my mom

Contents

Spurlos, 1970

THE PLACE SEEMED bigger and the paths wider, but maybe that was because of the weather. Usually things seem smaller when you grow out of them, but not the cemetery. It was endless.

Now it was spring, with a deep, wide-open sky and budding branches, and it wouldn't be long before we packed up our life on the army post in Germany and moved to Texas.

It seemed to me as if the time with Eliza had been a dream. She was my first best friend, and then she was gone. The way I remembered things shimmered and then grew dim. I tried to reach back and recall, but at every attempt I was blocked. The candy store we loved was shuttered. I made a trip to our place in the forest, Sebastian's Woods, but our precious "horse," a fallen tree, was completely different, with windfall branches blocking the perfect riding spot and evidence of more strangers, trespassers, smoking and drinking and sleeping in the woods. It felt dangerous.

So I went back to the cemetery because I thought maybe that would be the same.

Sure enough, there stood the pointy gates, the same as always. I walked along the paths now, because I was no longer running all the time, no longer riding an imaginary horse, which was what Eliza and I did. I had grown out of that. Now it seemed almost absurd to expend so much energy and move somewhere so quickly when I was not in a hurry. Maybe I was seeing into my future. If my birth was so close behind me, then maybe my death was not so far away in the other direction. I suddenly wanted everything to slow down. I was barely 14.

In the cemetery that day, I approached the bench in the alcove, where Eliza and I had retreated after entering the morgue that time. A woman was sitting there, and at first that startled me, and then when she turned her face toward me, I saw the familiar bright pink lips. We locked eyes in recognition. It was the woman from the candy store. Frau Jaw, we called her. She had been crying. I stopped and then was too embarrassed to walk on. The little dog, Spurlos, at the ground by her feet stood up and stared but did not bark. The woman stared too.

She had told me *"Vergessen Sie nicht,"* and, obeying, I had not forgotten. I had not forgotten anything. But meanwhile everything had changed.

I stood there on the gravel pathway like a statue, feeling the rush of time flow through me. Images passed across my field of vision. Eliza's blues, the smooshed pfennig, the floating feather, a crescent moon, and the white horse Kirsch, vanishing in the snow. The touchstones of my memory were so pure.

I remembered the woman's swollen eyes that day too, in the candy store, and how she had lost her cool. How Eliza and I mocked her then, made up stories at her expense. Now here she was in the cemetery, crying.

I smelled freshly turned dirt, and I looked over at a new grave decorated simply with a small urn of red carnations. It reminded me of my magnum champagne bottle stuffed with feather whips, now untouched, on a dusty corner of my dresser. Even after I gave Eliza a handful of whips to take when she left for Texas, I still had seven, one for each headstone in the baby graveyard.

I wanted to say something to Frau Jaw. I wanted her to know that I had not forgotten anything. I wanted to thank her for the chocolate candy, the Negerkussen, my first delicious kiss, because it was what I imagined true love to be: rare, dear, satisfying. But when I finally focused my eyes back on the bench, Frau Jaw and her little Spurlos were gone.

PART I

The Horse Show, 1970

ON SATURDAY MORNING, Gabby and I had tea and brotchen, but I ate only one bite with a few sips of tea before my stomach shut down. I was scared. We dressed in our breeches and shirts for the horse show and packed the car with all our stuff. We would hold off on the jackets and tall boots until right before the class. I felt sick, and the car ride made my nausea worse. I stared out the window, wishing this could be over. Mrs. Shore, Gabby's *Mutti,* was jabbering on about something, but I wasn't listening.

I mean, I was grateful that I got to ride. But I missed Eliza, and this new friend would never replace her.

When we got to the stables, I jumped out of the car and ran to Forella's stall. The force of the cold air in my lungs erased my tummyache, and then I breathed in the fragrance of the horse. Hugging Forella's neck, I knew I had to ride well for my little twin brothers, to show them on a horse what I instructed them to do when we play Horsey. I squeezed my eyes tight and made my promise to Forella, and she stood quietly, exuding warmth and calm.

Gabby was busy in the next stall grooming and tacking up Brav, so I came out of my reverie and got to work. I used a sturdy bristle brush for the first pass over Forella's copper coat and then followed it up with a large soft brush to shine her up. I used a miniature version of that brush to go over every inch of her face. She closed her eyes against my gentle strokes. Then I picked out her hooves, which were perfectly clean already, and saddled her. I had to reach up pretty high to get the saddle

4

positioned right, on the curve of her spine, with the fluffy pad laid smoothly beneath it. Then I tightened the girth gradually, with the plan of snugging it up once I was in the saddle.

The bridle leather felt smooth and well oiled in my hand and carried one of the notes in my favorite bouquet of fragrances. It included that rich saddle oil smell, vaporous horse breath, fresh hay, sweet molasses-covered oats, and the unlikely pleasing warm green scent of horse poop.

I held the bit in my fists for a minute to take off the chill and then set it at Forella's lips. She opened her jaw and took it, and I fitted the leather of the headstall over her head and behind her ears. She stood patiently so that I could move slow enough to prevent clanging the bit on her teeth. Once bridled, she lowered her head so that I could easily buckle everything up and pull her forelock free from the brow band. She needed that loose-forelock look.

To get to the show ring, we led the horses on a path around the big barn. I breathed deep with every step, staving off nausea. Then we waited in a holding paddock until our class was called. Not intentionally, Gabby and I mounted practically in unison, like some synchronized event, and that made me laugh. I got a pang of remembrance of how Eliza and I had pulled stunts like that, totally unpredictable and hilarious to us, serendipitous. Gabby was leaning over to tighten her girth, and I did the same. I adjusted my stirrups and slid my feet into them, sinking my knees low, feeling that familiar happy back-in-the-saddle feeling. We walked the horses around side by side to keep our nervousness at bay as the saddles warmed up beneath us. We talked nonsense, eager to laugh and diffuse tension, and generally tried to convince ourselves that the show was no biggie.

"We didn't even have to braid manes," said Gabby, which proved to us that it wasn't a fancy event. At the real high-end shows, the horses' coats and manes and tails are tamed into unnatural submission with scissors and razors and braids and elastics. But one of my favorite sights was a horse mane fluttering rhythmically at a canter, and that's what I would see when I looked down at Forella's neck.

Lots of other kids were taking the show too seriously. Some cried when they left the ring without a ribbon, their worried mothers following behind. I knew I would be one of those who didn't place, but there was no way I would cry. I was going to be thrilled it was over.

I looked up in the bleachers and saw where the Shores were sitting.

Mr. Shore was smoking a cigarette distractedly, and Mrs. Shore was reading a program. Then I noticed my mom with the twins, making their way along the crowded rows to sit next to Gabby's parents. Next thing I knew, though, Mrs. Shore had come in to the holding paddock with a small towel and was beckoning us over. She quickly buffed up Gabby's boots so that they were shiny and free of dust. Then she came over to clean mine too.

"You girls look great," she said, rubbing the length of my tall boot. "Good luck! Keep smiling!" Then she yanked my right foot from the stirrup and pulled at the stirrup leather, saying, "Philippa, your stirrups are uneven." Before I could explain, she adjusted the buckle up a hole, and then pulled the leather again, snapping the buckle back into place. She shoved my boot back into the stirrup. I didn't have a chance to redo it because she tapped Forella on the rump just as the voice on the loud-speaker called my class. Forella hopped forward, so I leaned toward her neck and talked softly to calm her down.

I had to enter the show ring with my right stirrup too short. Just that one hole was enough to make me uncomfortable and off-balance in the saddle. Mrs. Shore didn't know that I always ride with my stirrups uneven. It's the way I'm built. I guess she thought she was helping me by adjusting the length, but I needed that difference to make me even in the saddle. Now I was uneven, and the judge asked the class to advance to a trot right away so the whole herd of horses picked up speed around me. At least we were going around counter-clockwise, so my right leg was on the rail, unseen by the judge, who paced in the center of the ring with two assistants.

Forella's head was high, and I could tell she didn't appreciate the close quarters. Riders were negotiating their positions in the ring so they could be better noticed, so the clump of horses I was in finally began to thin out. Forella was going nicely, but my posting was abrupt and awk-ward. I couldn't get a nice rhythm because I was already so nervous and now the shorter stirrup was popping me up higher from the saddle than I wanted to go. I felt like an amateur, like people were laughing at me.

As I came around the ring to where my mom was, I caught eyes with the twins, and they were so excited to see me. Seeing their smiling faces, their fat red cheeks, helped me come out of myself momentarily and ride for them, stay true to Forella. The judge kept us at a working trot for several times around the arena, scrutinizing riders and making notes on her clipboard. I did my best to ignore her. I lost track of where Gabby was altogether.

Once, when I came around the arena again to where my mom was, I smiled briefly at her and then caught eyes with Mrs. Shore. She had her arms posed as if she were on horseback with reins in her hands. She was coaching me thumbs up. She was sitting with her back straight up and her hands positioned in fists. That was the way the Germans rode, and it was the hardest thing for me because none of my previous riding teachers had ever told me to hold my hands so staunchly thumbs up. Instead, I usually held my hands at a comfortable parallel to the horse's withers. But things were different in Germany, and I twisted my wrists so that my fists were perpendicular to the ground.

The combination of that adjustment and my uneven stirrups took away any grace that I felt I ever had in the saddle. My right leg felt cramped and my shoulders tight from trying to accommodate my seat to the adjusted stirrup. I couldn't clear my thoughts to keep my promise to Forella. I said to myself relax, relax, with each rise in the saddle as I posted, and just when I began to relax the judge ordered a canter, and the field of horses in the arena went haywire. Tails swishing, hooves kicking, riders holding on tight. It's not that the horses were misbehaving. It's just that when you have a contained space with lots of horses and riders of differing levels of competence, and all the horses are legged up into a canter at once, the result can be, let's say, exciting.

Forella moved into a canter with a couple of crow hops, and I sat them. They are kind of fun, like a little buck, but not if you lose your balance. I didn't. She stayed along the rail for me without much effort on my part. She seemed to sense the safety of it, there on the fringe. She cantered along in a collected manner, with her ears pricked forward, even though horses were going past us fast or cutting across the arena into a clear space. Sometimes a horse in front of us would balk or go too slow or even break into a trot. But I could easily maneuver Forella around, and she never broke from her canter. That horse was making me look good.

Somehow I managed to keep my seat by flexing my right heel down even deeper than usual so that my knee was positioned right in the knee roll and I had the best leverage in the saddle. But it was a strain on my seat overall, and I was beginning to tire. I hoped the judge would bring the field back down to a trot or even a walk, but it seemed like she was going to weed out the weak riders with this long canter. I began to breathe harder.

Then something happened that rocked my tiny bit of equilibrium. From the corner of my eye, I saw a dark streak coming across the arena. I turned my head to see a little runaway, and the rider was barely hanging on, trying to steer the horse and stop it at the same time, and not succeeding. The horse had bolted from a crowd, as if maybe the rider had wanted to head for a clearing in the arena. They veered toward Forella and cantered straight toward the rail. The rider wasn't in control at all. It was chaos coming toward me. I wanted to maintain the canter and guide Forella around the runaway, but it was too late. Another horse came up on my left and blocked my escape so that Forella had to hop to the right, and then she tossed up her head to stop before running into the little black horse, whose rider had fallen off into the dirt somewhere.

Forella's move was impossible for me to sit. I jounced to the left and immediately lost my right stirrup. Then when she ground to a halt with her head up, I flew forward against her neck and smashed my nose, and then I tumbled over her right shoulder into the metal railing. My arm banged into the rail and I slammed onto the ground. I looked up into swirling dust and flashing horseshoes. I saw my outstretched fingers and the underside of Forella's chin in disparate images. Forella didn't step on me. Then suddenly the horses were gone and I was alone in a heap.

I looked up. All the riders stopped their horses and dismounted so that there was no activity in the ring at all. I peeked up from under my armpit and saw someone helping the runaway's rider from the ring. She was limping and crying, wailing really. I smelled the sweet metallic blood flowing from my nose. I saw my mom running across the arena toward me and shut my eyes, willing this to be a nightmare from which I would awaken in my featherbed at home. But when I reopened them, it was real.

"Philippa! Are you alright?" My mom kneeled down beside me and rolled me over onto my back. "Let me see you! Look at me!"

"Mom, I'm okay. Oww!" My ribs hurt. My arm hurt. "Where's Forella?"

"Gabby has her. She's okay," said my mom. "Come on, let's get you up."

I felt so embarrassed. I couldn't believe I had fallen off in front of the twins. But when I stole a glance their way, I saw them smiling. I realized that to them it wasn't such a big deal. At their age, you fall down all the time. It's just part of your life, not something bad or embarrassing. You just get back up. And I did.

Someone led Forella back to me, and I mounted up and finished the class, after readjusting my stirrup, of course. But I didn't place because of the fall. And Gabby didn't place either. Her mom was angry about it, at first at the judge, who, she said, was obviously incompetent, and then at Gabby.

On the drive home, Mutti told Gabby, "You vere posting like a jack-in-ze-box," her English accented with German. I regretted not having begged my mom to take me home with her, but she didn't offer it as an option so I figured she was busy and wanted me to stay out for the weekend as arranged. And then Mutti criticized her daughter's hands and her feet and the fact that Gabby hadn't been smiling the whole time. I tried to disappear in the car seat during Mrs. Shore's tirade, and Mr. Shore said nothing, smoking what seemed like a whole pack before we pulled into the garage at their home.

IT WAS EARLY evening, but I could tell that no one was planning on preparing dinner. No wurst tonight, which was fine with me. Both parents vanished to separate parts of the house, and Gabby and I rustled around in the kitchen for bread and cheese and milk and chocolate. We piled it on a tray, brought it to her room, and set it up between us on the bed.

We carefully avoided the topic of the show at first, both feeling self-conscious. The house was so quiet. I wasn't used to this sort of family, with the parents so obviously at odds, in some sort of silent conflict. I was used to being cared for by my mom, her making me meals, and by a lot of activity when my dad was home, with the twins and all. I guess Gabby was used to this awkward stillness, being an only child. I bet she was glad to have me there for company.

We had finished our cheese and bread and were playing with a German chocolate bar. We broke it into small squares along the scores and then held the pieces between our fingers until enough melted to coat our fingertips. Then we licked the chocolate from our fingers.

"I could easily live on chocolate alone," I said.

9

"Mm-hm," agreed Gabby.

"Well, chocolate and horses," I said.

Gabby laughed. "You could live on horses?" She thought that was really funny. Maybe it was in the translation, I don't know. So I went with it.

"Yes, I could. I could sleep on them and eat on them, but forget about showing on them," I said.

Gabby's mood changed, and she flopped over on her side, disrupting our tray so that one of the milk glasses fell over.

"*Ach,* I hate those shows," she said. "I never do what Mutti likes. Even when I place, it's not enough."

"But you're such a good rider on Brav," I said.

"*Ja,* but not good enough for Mutti," she said.

Then we were quiet for a while, and I set the glass back up. Gabby got off the bed and went to close the bedroom door. She turned toward me with a sly grin, her back against the closed door: "Want to see something?"

She came back to her side of the bed and slid open the door of the cabinet in the headboard. I was surprised to see an old wooden box in there, and Gabby pulled it out. I thought of Eliza's box that reminded her of good things, and I guessed this would be the same type of thing. But it wasn't decorated like Eliza's box, and I got a whiff of tobacco and ashes.

Gabby didn't hesitate. She slid open the lid and pulled out a pack of cigarettes.

"This is what I do when they get like that," she said, gesturing with her chin toward the door, toward her parents in other parts of the house. She was awkward with the cigarette, holding it deep in the crotch of two fingers. She wrapped her lips around her teeth and set the cigarette in her mouth like that. Then she struggled to light the match, striking it several times, her face serious in concentration, and then when it lit, she yelped and dropped it in a panic into the cigar box and then frantically dug it out while blowing on it.

I sat there saying nothing. On one level it seemed funny. On another, pathetic. Finally I said, "What are you doing?"

Gabby ignored me and began the process again, this time a little calmer and with some success. Her fingers in a V, she secured the cigarette in her mouth, lit it, and pulled. Then she had a mouthful of smoke and didn't know what to do with it. She didn't want to inhale it. I could tell she wasn't pleased with the taste. Then she spoke up, releasing the stinking smoke at once, saying, "You want one?"

"No!" I said, almost too quickly. "I would never..."

I was astounded, and I could not imagine smoking, much less having a box full of cigarettes and matches hidden away. I mean, smoking was for another kind of girl. Gabby immediately snuffed out the cigarette and threw it in the box, hastily closing it just as there was a knock on the door.

We both froze, staring at each other. Then I saw her expression change in the most minuscule way. Maybe her brows adjusted or maybe the edge of her mouth twitched, I don't know, but I could tell from her expression she was begging me to help, to make it right. I let a moment slip by.

Mrs. Shore called out in a muted tone: "Gabriella? *Liebschen?*"

I could hear a change in Mrs. Shore's tone too, like she wasn't angry anymore, like she wanted to make up with her daughter. But if she came in now, she would discover Gabby's secret. The room reeked. I could see a haze drifting in the air. She would be mad at me too, at both of us, and she would tell my mom and then I would never get to ride Forella again. I had to do something.

"I'm dressing!" I said.

Gabby's eyebrows went up, and her lips parted.

"One minute, Mutti," Gabby said, her voice soft and babyish, ready to be conciliatory.

"Okay, zat's okay," said Mrs. Shore. She sounded relieved. "See you in ze morning." Her voice had turned singsong and playful.

"Okay, goodnight," said Gabby.

"Goodnight, Mrs. Shore," I said. "Thank you."

Gabby and I sat staring at each other. Moments went by.

"Thanks," she said, finally.

"It's okay," I said. Then with an edge on my voice, "I don't know about that box."

I felt myself scolding her, like I was better than her and needed to tell her what to do. She could hear it in my voice and wasn't having any of it.

"That's good," she said, smugly, closing the headboard cabinet. Then she turned it all around on me. "You *don't* know anything about it."

Gabby pulled down the covers to get into bed.

"So let's forget about it, okay?" she said and let out a little cough.

11

She seemed to have gotten so angry so quickly. Then I coughed too and got under the covers. Gabby shut out the lamp, but I laid awake for a good while, longing for my own bed and my own warm feather blanket.

12

Smoke in the Woods

THE NIGHT IS so cold that I can't even feel it. I am numb on the outside, but I feel something painful inside that I want to escape. So I keep walking in the snow, into the cold night, the night that is both black and white.

I know where to go, and if I keep walking I can keep breathing the wicked cold air and keep not feeling the cold. I finger the matchbox deep in the left pocket of my cords. Now my feet have turned to ice from breaking through drifts of snow. On top of the drifts the snow seems illuminated, catching a glint from the moon; in the valleys the snow is bruised purple-black.

Lights glow in the windows of houses, but that's not where I am going. I am going into the woods.

In Germany you are always going into the woods. My life has been cut from the woods. My house, the roads, the school, the hospital—all cut from the woods.

Not the cemetery, though. It seems to be part of the woods, with no border.

Behind the hospital is a dense section of woods, with two paths that cut a V toward the building. One path takes you straight to the rear entrance; the other directs you left, around the building. The hospital people don't want us kids to walk through the hospital on the way to school. We are supposed to go around, to the left.

Tonight I am breaking rules, going straight into the hospital, to the basement, where I can pull cigarettes from the vending machine

13

and smoke them to warm my lungs.

I have only just started smoking, so I won't die from it yet.

The woods are scary, more at night than in the day. In the day, the contrast between daylight and the gloom of the forest is startling. I become jumpy. At night, everything is dark and spooky. Tonight is different, and I am not afraid. Now the woods behind the hospital are welcoming, pulling me closer to what I want.

I have brought along coins, American coins, and the hospital basement is deserted. It is so late that the little PX store is closed and that military police guy who busted me before is nowhere to be seen, which is good. He would be onto me in a minute.

I insert the coins into the vending machine, and they clink and echo as if the entire machine is empty, but I know it's not. I pull the knob, and filterless Peter Stuyvesants tumble into my grasp. I quickly climb the stairs, hiding the pack from view. I escape the basement of the hospital, exit the building, and get back into the arms of the woods.

My fingers are practically useless in this cold. My bare arms didn't warm up in the building. I fumble to open the pack and drop pieces of wrapper onto the forest floor.

I remove a cigarette and pocket the pack. My match ignites instantly on the first stroke and glows like the windows of houses. I place the flame to the tip of the cigarette. The tobacco is sweet on my tongue. I pull in the smoke, inhale, gag, and cough. My chest cramps, and I drop to the ground, hanging my head. My hair is a curtain in the night. I wait a beat. Then I bring the cigarette back to my lips and try again.

Better this time. I can do this. All it takes is a little getting used to. Again. There. Better. I get a dizzy rush. What would Eliza think if she saw me now?

Munich, Germany, 1969

WHEN WE MOVED into the house in Munich, it seemed as if we had been there before. But we hadn't. It's just that all army post houses look alike, inside and out. Even my twin brothers ran around the house as if they were familiar with the rooms and the furniture. All the furniture was beige and neutral, and the house smelled like the corner of a closet, as if it had been closed up too long.

"Boys!" my mother called as August and Quinn bounded up the steep stairs, using their arms and hands as if they were horses climbing a bluff. "Philippa, bring them back down, would you, please? We haven't got much time here today. I just wanted to take a quick look."

I hurried up the curving wooden staircase after the five-year-olds, mimicking their climbing technique, and found them bouncing about on the big bed in the master bedroom. The impact of their little bodies on the bed created a trampoline effect, and their giggles became contagious.

"Guys, come on," I said, trying to be serious and authoritative but failing. They could hear my voice break, and I tumbled onto the bed with them. I pulled a fatigue-green army blanket from the foot of the bed, threw it over them like a net, and captured the little monsters. That got them going, and the woolen blanket came alive with them laughing beneath it. Faces appeared, now ruddy with exertion, and I grabbed the boys each around the middle, putting my fingers between their ribs as if playing two plump accordions, and they squealed louder.

"Philippa! Bring them down," I heard my mother call. Her voice had a strain to it, but not the type of strain when a person is yelling to be heard. There was an edge to it, of annoyance, like she was impatient. I didn't want to irritate her any more than she already was. So I pulled to a sitting position on the edge of the bed, still clutching the boys. August and Quinn leaped from my grasp and ran ahead of me down the hall and to the staircase. They disappeared, and my stomach lurched.

"Hold the railing," I said in my best adult-sounding voice as I strode down the hall, taking in the four bedrooms and two bathrooms on the second story of the house. I heard the boys clamoring down the stairs and caught up with them midway, just as the staircase turned its corner, so that my mother would think I had safely supervised them all the way down.

"What do you think of this unique chair, Philippa?" she asked, leaning on its back. I could tell she was trying to be nice in spite of her mood. She was making a joke, because in fact this chair was exactly like one we had had in a previous house, huge and rounded, covered with a coarse dirt-colored fabric. My mother despised that furniture. But its thick back was perfect for straddling like a horse. She often draped the backs of dull chairs with bright batiks or textured throws, which in my reality were saddles.

"Oh, it's lovely," I answered with sort of an accent, to play along, pretending not to have noticed her previous tone of voice, and I grabbed the boys' hot sticky hands as we headed out the door.

We had moved to Germany in early summer. I was 13. My entire life had been a series of moves from army post to post, so it wasn't unusual for me to have to become accustomed to a new place. Since I never knew a different way of life, I didn't mind the constant moves.

My mother grew to hate it. She resented the disorganization that constant moving brought. She needed a state of calm and quiet to work. She wrote poetry and who knows what all else, not for books or anything, just for herself, she told me. She never showed it to me. She said it helped her make sense of things. But moving disrupted her work. The more distant she got from writing, the more distant she got from me.

This was the first foreign country that we had lived in, though, with a completely different culture and language, so I could tell she tried to be open-minded. On the post, I would go to an American school, but still, I could feel that we were foreigners. It added complexity to the move, and I found myself becoming more moderate and compliant, to fit in my family and cause no friction. I needed the security.

I took on a lot of responsibility for the twins, especially when we moved to a new post. My mother had come to expect it of me, she said, because she hadn't expected to have the twins. I guess she had been happy with one child, me, and hadn't planned on getting pregnant again. In addition to having twin boys to care for, she would have her hands full with the logistics of the move. Daddy would start his new job at the post hospital, and that occupied him fully. He was gone a lot.

So I looked after the twins and helped get their meals and, as they grew bigger, played with them. Their favorite game was Horsey, with me on my hands and knees and them climbing on and off and falling to the ground when I bucked. It was an exhausting game, but it allowed me to enter the fantasy world that I had created in anticipation of someday having my own horse.

I knew I would have my own horse but not until we had settled in one place. As Daddy always said, "Military life is not stable, and how can you have a horse with no stable?" He and Mom both smiled blandly at that but not to mock me. It was because this was a fact of our life, that I'd have to wait.

Now that we were in Munich, I found myself clinging ever more tightly to the twins. I had one of their little-boy hands for each of mine, and it gave me a feeling of safety and a feeling of purpose.

Whatever happened in this new place, I knew August and Quinn needed me and would always look up to me with their wide-set dark eyes and smooth brows. Even if I didn't have a best friend, they would be my friends, they would be my back-up, my safety net. I knew how to care for them even if I messed up in school, got confused, forgot things. Maybe, if we were lucky, we would stay here for more than just one year and I could make some friends. But, I cautioned myself, I shouldn't set my expectations too high. It was better to take things as they came and take pleasure in small things first.

WHEN I FIRST met Eliza, it was late summer. I was sitting in a bright green patch of clover in the lawn behind the house, and the twins were napping. The windows to their bedroom were open, and I could see the curtains flutter. I imagined the dark quiet of the room. The sun was warm on my back, but underneath the clover the ground was cool and moist, and I pushed my bare feet around so that the clover slid between my toes.

We had moved to Munich from Los Angeles, where we lived for a year, hardly long enough for me to get my bearings on the place. There had been a restlessness, an undercurrent that even I, as a young girl, could feel. The war in Vietnam was the reason. Teenage boys were fighting there and dying, and there were protests.

Before L.A. we had spent three long warm sunny years in Hawaii, where I went to school barefooted and we spent Christmas on the beach. I rode horses in the mountains and picked guavas high in trees from the vantage point of horseback. Today in Munich, the weather was balmy, like those Hawaiian days, and I had no worries.

I was grazing an expensive bone china palomino horse figurine of my mother's. It was my habit to bring horse statues out to the lawn and enter a miniature world where the horses grazed in greenery up to their bellies. The statues were only about five inches tall. They were wild horses, free to run wherever they wanted. No one ever captured them because they were too fast and clever.

"Philippa?" It was my mom. "Philippa, where are you?" Where else would I be? I hadn't started my explorations yet; I was staying close to home.

"I'm out here." Then they came into view around the side of the house. My mother was walking with a man, and he was holding the hand of a girl my age. She was blond and pretty. She wore her hair long and parted down the middle, like I did.

"Philippa, this is Dr. Romin and his daughter Eliza," said my mom. I caught the fragrance of pipe smoke. The man was gray at the temples, and he let go of the girl's hand, moving behind her. "Dr. Romin and Daddy work together at the hospital."

I knew that already from my parents' dinner conversations. Eliza's dad was the boss of the hospital, and my dad was a doctor there. When they discovered they had daughters the same age, they decided to introduce us. I had wondered what this girl would be like, but I hadn't gotten my hopes up.

I stood up to face Eliza, and she looked steadily at me with blue eyes and said hi. She wasn't as tall as I was. Then she turned her attention to my horse in the clover and dropped down to look more closely.

"I love palominos," she said. "This is beautiful. The palomino is my favorite color, and then the bay and, next, the dapple gray."

I was so glad Eliza wasn't shy. I didn't have time for that. I sat down Indian-style across from her.

"Dapple gray is my favorite, and then bay, and then palomino," I said. "Kind of the mirror opposite of you."

"Do you have a gray statue?" she said. "I have one that is rearing up. We can go to my house and get it. I have a bay foal too."

By then our parents had wandered back to the house, their heads lowered in conversation.

"Let's say the palomino is the bay's mom," I said, pulling on my shoes.

"Okay. But let's say the foal is weaned already," said Eliza, and we took off toward her house.

Eliza lived in the colonel's quarters, which were larger houses than the duplexes where I lived, but it was only a short walk away. The military post also had lots of apartments. When I went inside Eliza's house, it seemed the same as mine, only bigger. And there was all the same furniture.

No one was home, and the place was quiet.

"Where's your mom?" I asked.

"My mom doesn't live here," she said.

I wondered why. I expected more of an explanation, but instead Eliza took the stairs by twos. The staircase went straight up and didn't curve like the one in my house.

Eliza shared her room with her older sister. She also had two older brothers. She was the baby of the family, and you could tell, because her bed had a bunch of cute stuffed animals and dolls and her shelves were full of horse statues that were running and rearing and grazing and posing. Sometimes when I looked away, they shimmered in the corner of my eye.

"See, here's the gray stallion," said Eliza, carefully taking him down from the shelf. "He is always protecting the herd. Let's take him and the foal and then these two mares too."

We arranged the horses into a herd on the wooden floor. Their hooves made a nice *clickety-clack* when they cantered.

"Are your parents divorced?" I asked.

"What? No. My mom is sick, and she has to be taken care of all the time," said Eliza.

"What's wrong with her?"

"It's something . . . she's . . ."

I realized I had gone too far. And by the tone of Eliza's voice, I also began to feel like I didn't want to know. It was something she was having trouble expressing, so I knew it wasn't good. But it felt too awkward not to say anything, and I kept going.

"So, is she . . ."

"She lives in the hospital, and I visit her there," said Eliza, with finality.

"Oh." Then we stopped talking and moved our various statues through grazing and rolling and trotting until the conversation came back.

"Do you like goomey bears?" asked Eliza. Her voice showed no signs of discomfort or emotion. She had left the previous conversation behind, and I was relieved.

"Goomey bears..." I said. "What are they?"

"You've never had a goomey bear?" she said, and she hopped up onto her bed.

On her bedside table, Eliza had a small box that she had decorated with pictures from magazines, like pictures of horses and other animals, and things in pretty colors, like little jewels and sparkly tassels and feathers and stuff like that. I joined her on the bed, and she opened the lid of the box. When she opened it, a nice smell came out, like the cherry vanilla pipe smoke smell, from her dad. Inside was a collection that she said reminded her of good things.

For instance, there were ticket stubs and a bracelet and a marble and dried flowers and a halfway-burned candle and some photos and other stuff that I couldn't clearly see—but she wasn't intending for me to look at all of it anyway. It was private. She pulled out a little white paper bag, closed the box, and then dumped a bunch of colorful soft jelly candies from the bag onto her bed. I had never seen them before, so they were somewhat alluring. We didn't have them in the States. I later discovered they were spelled "gummi," and then years later, when they made it to the U.S., Americans pronounced their name like "gum."

"These are goomey bears," she said. "What's your favorite color?"

"Purple."

"Same here," she said, curling up one side of her mouth, looking as if she already knew we had that in common. Then she looked at the pile of candy. "What's your favorite of these colors?"

"Okay, red," I said. The goomey bears were red, green, kind of a clear white, orange, and yellow. Eliza picked out a few red ones and handed them to me.

"Try them. I'll take you to the goomey store and we can get some more, okay?" she said. "It'll be fun. We'll get a bunch and then make trades with each other."

Then after I had popped a goomey in my mouth, she asked, "So, what do you think?"

"Pretty good," I told her, but I was secretly hoping this wasn't the best candy Germany had to offer. I needed something with more substance. Something creamy and chocolate.

"No, I mean about going to the goomey store and making trades," she said.

"Sounds cool," I answered, but really what I was thinking was that I had a best friend now. And I wouldn't trade that for anything.

Just as I was about to stuff a couple more red goomey bears in my mouth, Eliza looked up as if she expected something to happen, and then it did. We heard the front door open and then slam shut, and a man's voice yelled, "Eliza? Eliza, come down!"

"Coming, Daddy!" she said, and she bounded off the bed and out the door. I went as fast as I could to follow. When I got to the top of the stairs, I saw Eliza and her dad at the bottom. He was saying something to her, but I couldn't tell what, and then she looked up at me and grabbed the front doorknob at the same time.

"I gotta go! Would you put my horses up for me?" she said. "I'll see you later, okay?" And both Eliza and her dad slipped out the front door, leaving me alone.

"Okay," I said into the echoing stairwell, and I turned to her room to put the horses back safely where they belonged.

Running in the Woods

ELIZA AND I have split. And with her went everything that made me happy. A best friend, running through the woods, running through the woods with a best friend. Now I walk these frozen trails alone, and tonight I am piecing together the past so that I can recover something, anything from it.

I remember kissing Stefan like it was now. I don't like it, though, him pushing toward me, to devour me. His face is small, framed in shaggy brown hair, but his eyes are wide and open. The skin of his face touches mine as he brushes closer. It feels like fine sandpaper. I like that.

Stefan likes me and he's nice to me. He understands how I love his horses, and we sit close to them, beneath their muzzles while they chew their hay. We laugh at how prehistoric their mouths look, when you look at their lips, the way they wiggle with hay sticking out. When Stefan wants to kiss me, I run away. I remember it too like it was now. And now when I remember, I wish I had stayed.

But I didn't know what I know now. Stefan needed me, like a boy needs a girl. That scared me. It was too much for me, more than I need. I need the horses, their warmth, their fragrance. They are large good creatures, the purest good. I understand them. I don't understand boys.

Stefan is chained to the traveling carnival and his pony concession. He does his family's work, and that is all he'll ever do. He wants to stay in Munich with me, or so he says, and I begin to feel like I want to go away with him, moving through Germany in the carnival. His mother clutches him. Mine ignores me.

I am thinking more clearly now, but my ears are squeezing my skull with enough force to crack it. Might be the nicotine, but it's probably just the cold. Or maybe it is the thought of going back home. I cannot stand the thought of those looks my parents give me, those disgusted, disappointed looks. And the stern talk. There is no yelling, just stern talk about how disappointed they are in the behavior that shows how ungrateful I am for all they have done for me.

I place the cigarette to my lips again and pull. There. Better. I exhale a plume of smoke, and I like to watch it dissolve and disappear. I shudder, then I notice I am shivering. I am sweating. I turn toward home, where my house is cut from the woods.

But I don't really want to go home. I would rather keep walking the trails in the woods before they are all obscured by snow. I wish I could run those trails again, like Eliza and I used to, but everything is different now and I'd hardly know where to turn.

The cigarette has burned down short, and when it singes my fingers I throw it down. It sizzles in the snow, and I hiss back. I feel a snarl curl my lips yet my hands find their way back into my pockets for another. The pack is somewhat crushed, but I manage to get a cigarette out unbroken.

I am wearing my pants a lot tighter now than I used to, back when Eliza and I ran the forest trails together. I peg my cords. Everybody does it. You can make them really tight so that they are hard to get on, to get your foot through. But they look good. They look real different from when they were baggy. It is the way all the girls wear them now. My mom says it is absurd, but I don't care.

I am not wearing a coat. That is because I have no coat. I refuse to buy a new coat even though my old one was too small, my purple maxi coat. My mom wanted to take me shopping for another, but I did not want to go. Then she just got rid of it, my favorite purple maxi coat. She has this odd habit of discarding things like clothes in a really knee-jerk reaction sort of way, because you never know when we might be posted somewhere else, and why have too much flotsam and jetsam to deal with? So she got rid of it. That was my favorite coat. It was deep dark purple. It was just like Eliza's.

The woods have opened up now into a place where there is more housing, mostly apartment buildings. Circles of lamplight brighten the snow. I walk through that exposed area quickly, heading toward the end of the post where the Little Oktoberfest carnival sets up.

Hardly anyone is out so late tonight; I shouldn't be out so late. I see just one or two people now and then, probably soldiers switching shifts, hurrying to get out of the cold. Their presence is not comforting. They seem like shadows. When my mom discovers me gone, her head will spin, but that will serve her right for being so mean.

I come to a thick section of woods cut with paths, and I have run these paths before on my way to the Little Oktoberfest, with the twins running ahead of me like frisky colts. Tonight, though, I am only plodding along, trying to go back and find something inside the ring of worn earth that the ponies trod round and round every day.

The footpaths of the Oktoberfest are etched onto the hard, cold ground. Most of the rides are packed up for leaving tomorrow. Or when the weather is less ominous. No one is out. There is the worn-down midway, now covered in snow. Some parts of the land were never trampled, like the section where the big twirling swing ride stood, still covered with dried grass that is long enough to peek through the snow. And here is the pony concession, a big obvious circle, and I stoop down to scratch up a few bits of sawdust. The arena with its ring of twinkling lights is dismantled.

I pull out my pack and sit cross-legged in the dead center of the circle. Just as I light one, I imagine one of Jurgen's cigarette stubs. He was always tossing his butts into the dirt, and he did not always stomp them cold with his big black boot. Sometimes they smoldered. Stefan hated that about his brother. Fire is dangerous around horses. I take a drag, not too deep. I have figured out that short and shallow is better.

My friendship with Eliza is over. There is nothing I can do about that, and it aches. I will not make that mistake again—get so close. I didn't with Stefan. I remember now. I know he is leaving. He cannot escape the carnival and stay in Munich with me. He has to take care of the ponies because he cannot depend on Jurgen, because Jurgen is a drinker.

I can picture Jurgen: He slumps in a chair in the corner of the trailer, his big black boots splayed before him, buffed, aggressively cleaned of manure before he enters. The only work he does is crack the whip, and that makes him so tough. Stefan does everything else.

Stefan tells me Mutti begs him to stay. And he will. He must. But he loves me, he tells me. He is so beautiful when he says it, so sincere. I see his lips move, but I cannot hear it. How can he love me? I think he says he loves me only because I can turn around and run away, into the arms of the woods.

The Goomey Lady, 1969

"MOM, WHAT'S WRONG with Eliza's mother?" I asked that night as I tore lettuce for the dinner salad.

"Hmm?" she said. She was stirring spaghetti sauce at the stove, and I could tell her mind was elsewhere, probably busy solving poetry problems. Thinking of rhymes. I don't know. Once I watched her get up from a chair where she was writing, with her papers in her hands, her head bent to them, reading, walk to the refrigerator, open it, pull out a half-drunk glass of red wine from the night before, close the fridge door with her foot, and go back to work in her chair, and never look up that whole time. I learned not to take her distraction personally. I reached for a carrot to grate.

"Eliza's mom is in the hospital. When is she getting out?"

"I don't know," she said, turning toward me. A chunk of her dark hair had escaped from the bobby pins that held most of it back, and she reached to push it behind her ear. "You'll have to ask Daddy. Maybe he knows."

But by the time Daddy got home from the hospital, the question had dropped from my mind. During the meal, my mom and dad carried on a conversation that became a droning sound to me while I ate. Every now and then I wanted to say something, but I didn't. My parents did not take well to interruptions in their conversation. Even August and Quinn knew that, and they were only five.

Finally the conversation turned a corner and I heard my name, so I tuned in. We had to buy some warmer clothes, they were saying, because the weather was going to get cold. Plus I always got to buy something special for the first day of school.

Ugh, the dreaded first day of school—a vast open space in which I had no idea what to expect. I felt panic and excitement pulling on me from either side like the twins do sometimes, when they both want a part of me. No one's face would be familiar, everything would smell new and different and nauseating, and the hallways would be confusing mazes, with me, a little lost mouse, running around disoriented.

I had done this before—started at a new school—but it never got easier. Everyone but me seemed to know the way around. And they all seemed to know each other. All I could rely upon were the familiar rhythms of my own body, and that was not always very comfortable. For one thing, I was usually nauseated for the first few hours of the first few days. I would drag myself to school and struggle through the morning until finally I would feel hungry instead of sick.

For the first time, though, I lived close enough to school so that I could walk home for lunch, and my mom promised to make something familiar for me. Soup and a sandwich and some potato chips and some sweet canned fruit, maybe.

Eliza and I had a few weeks to enjoy before we started eighth grade, so we took full advantage of the free time to explore the post and even off the post. Eliza showed me all her usual hangouts and, of course, the goomey store. A tall, serious woman worked there, and we called her the goomey lady. We bought sticky candies and then ran home with our little white paper bags of junk to trade on the wooden floor upstairs. Sometimes Eliza took something from her decorated box, like another color goomey snake to trade.

We were always running off somewhere, because in our imaginations we were always on horses. My horse was a light dapple gray, with an extremely long black mane and tail. She was a mare, and I called her Flyer. Eliza's horse, also a mare, was a golden palomino with a white mane and tail. Her tail was thick and trimmed straight across at the bottom so it didn't drag on the ground. Eliza named her Posey.

"Okay, let's review the numbers," said Eliza. She knew German numbers because she had been in Munich a year already. We were planning a trip to the goomey store with the twins, strategizing in the front yard of my house. The goomey store was off the post across a high-traffic road, over the city tram tracks, and on the far side of a gully. I could not imagine how Eliza had found it, but I figured it was one of those secrets passed along through friends. The goomey lady did not speak English, and Eliza told me she was freaky and unpredictable.

"*Eins, zwei, drei, vier,*" I said, counting to four.

"Good," said Eliza. "If you want more than four of anything, just give me the sign."

"The sign?"

"Yeah, you know. Just hold up all five fingers. And you two," she said, turning her attention to the twins. "Do you like goomey bears?" Somehow she had pulled both boys up onto her hips, one on each side. The twins adored Eliza from the moment they met. She was so well loved by her family that she knew how to give it all back, and the twins could feel it.

"I want all the yellow goomey bears," Quinn said, clapping his hands. His dark eyes were bright and eager. Quinn's hair was a shade darker than August's, but both boys had unruly beach-blond hair.

"What about you, August?"

"Come on, horsey, giddy-up," he said. He wanted to be carried.

I helped Eliza wriggle August around behind her so that he could ride Horsey, and then I hoisted Quinn up onto my back by first setting him astraddle on my hip and then shifting him around to the back, above my rump. And off we went to the goomey store, the pockets of our baggy corduroys stuffed with pfennigs.

"*Hyah, hyah, hyah,*" yelled August, flapping his arms down in an attempt to whip Eliza's butt.

When we walked through the front door of the goomey store, a little black dog began yapping like crazy, standing in one place as if his tiny pointy paws were glued to the floor. August and Quinn were both off our backs by then, and they cowered around my legs even though the dog would probably be no match for a rat.

"Guys, it's just a little pup," I said to them, and bent over to approach the yapping dog. But then the door to the back room opened a crack and the goomey lady slinked through like a cat, her eyes zig-zagging among all four of us. She pulled on a faded turquoise-blue cardigan in one graceful motion as she appeared in the room. Staring at the dog, she said through gritted teeth, "Spurlos..." The dog immediately shut up. I abandoned the idea of petting it.

The room became deadly quiet in the presence of the goomey lady. She had a broad face, small dark eyes, and short black hair, and she wore bright pink lipstick in a thick swath on her lips. She stood behind a large glass case along the back wall of the store. Actually she towered behind the case, because she was a giant and she looked like she was standing guard. She must have looked even bigger to the twins. Plus, she did not smile with those bright pink lips. She just stood behind the candy case waiting for us to decide what we wanted, impatient for us to get our transaction completed and leave. The boys stayed close to me, with the entire lengths of their bodies pressed against my legs.

"Drei Schlangen, bitte," I said, breaking the silence by asking for three goomey snakes. Other choices were the goomey bear, of course, and the little goomey Coke bottles and the goomey pacifiers. I hoped for at least one red one, but there was no chance requesting a color. Eliza said you get what the goomey lady gives, and do not even make an issue of it. Eliza said once she asked for green and the goomey lady dumped back all the goomeys she had already put in Eliza's bag, stood back from the counter, and raised her hands up as if to say, "No more." Eliza had to leave without any candy.

I chose a few other goomeys, and then I let the twins point to what they wanted. The goomey lady stiffened as she eyed the finger smears they left on the glass case. After Eliza made her selections, we took turns paying, and then the goomey lady folded up the bags and handed them to us.

"Danke," Eliza and I said together. The goomey lady just looked at us, still not smiling. She seemed to be not all there, as if she was thinking about something else and using us as comparison. I felt like a bug under a microscope.

Let's get out of here, I thought. Then I noticed a tray of chocolate candies on a shelf behind the glass case. The candies were about the size of eggs, and the tray looked like an egg carton, but bigger and without a lid. I had to know what they were, even though the twins were pulling on my cords and trying to move me in the direction of the door. I had to ask.

"Was ist das?" I said, using my elementary German, and the goomey lady turned toward the shelf, following my pointed finger. I sensed Eliza staring at me. She wanted out of there.

"Hier?" the goomey lady asked, lightly touching the tray of candies.

"Ja."

"Negerkussen," she announced, and her eyebrows arched upward.

"How much?" I said, not knowing the German for it and hoping the goomey lady could gather my meaning. I sensed that these Negerkussen might be the kind of candy I was looking for. After all, they were covered in chocolate.

The goomey lady stood expressionless for a moment and then resituated the price sign so that I could see it, and I began to calculate how many I could buy. When I looked up from the coins in my hand, I saw that she had removed one Negerkusse and was holding it in her hand for me to look at. She held it right in front of my face, and I focused on its plump bell shape. Beyond its darkness I could see the blur of her pink lips. I wondered what was under the chocolate, straining to burst out. I glanced at Eliza to see if she knew anything about this candy, but she looked as surprised as I. Four little hands were still tugging at my pants.

"Hold on, guys," I said to the twins, and then I looked back up at the goomey lady.

With all our attention on her, she raised the Negerkusse to her eye level in an exaggerated dramatic fashion and said, *"Schokolade."* There was complete quiet, and her statement needed no translation. I did not take my eyes off of her. I couldn't. It looked like something was going to happen. Even the boys were transfixed. Up close I could see delicate dark hairs above her upper lip. I could hear Eliza's soft breathing.

Then the goomey lady brought the Negerkusse to her lips, pursing them tightly, and kissed it. She actually kissed the Negerkusse. I envisioned a puckered pink stamp on the glossy surface of the chocolate. And then she said, *"Kusse."*

I felt my scalp tingle, and I felt an urge to laugh. Somehow I stifled it, but the twins both started giggling and Eliza kneeled down beside them and tried to quiet them. Spurlos began yapping again.

None of the commotion stopped the goomey lady. She was on a roll. Next she opened her mouth wide, like her jaw came unhinged. Her large pink lips stretched like an overblown balloon, and she placed the entire Negerkusse in her mouth. Then she slowly bit down on it. Her eyes became little happy slits, and even though her lips stayed tightly together as she worked her jaw, they formed into a smile, and her cheeks puffed up right below her eyes.

"Vier, bitte," I said between dog yaps, asking for four, hoping she would stop with the dramatics. I struggled with my change, trying to

concentrate on counting the money and helping Eliza hang onto the boys at the same time. Eliza noticed I was short, and she handed me a couple of coins. Then she grabbed the boys' hands and headed for the door. The goomey lady placed my Negerkussen into a white bag and handed it to me. She glared at Spurlos, and he quieted and slunk away. She turned to me.

"Vergessen Sie nicht," she said, telling me not to forget. She looked at me as if she was telling me a life secret. "Negerkussen."

"Negerkussen," I repeated, holding her gaze and trying to be respectful, while Eliza pushed the boys through the door. I stood a moment, and as the goomey lady turned toward her room, I repeated "Negerkussen" to myself. *Don't forget,* I thought, and pulled myself back to the present.

The minute the heavy door closed behind us, Eliza and I fell against the building, gasping for air. Quinn grabbed at my white bag, trying to get a Negerkusse. Then we all ran up the embankment toward the road. Once we were out of earshot of the goomey store, we let loose with laughter and sucked in the cold blue air. Then we found a place to sit cross-legged, on a ledge back away from the tracks, and I pulled out a Negerkusse for each of us.

The guys immediately bit into theirs and became completely involved. What I mean is that they were covered in Negerkusse. I held mine in my palm, and Eliza copied me, so I went with her mood, playing the goomey lady. We pursed our lips, straining against the urge to laugh, and kissed our candies.

"Kusse!" we blurted and shoved the Negerkussen into our mouths. We sat in silence as we let the dreamy things dissolve on our tongues.

"Mmmm," murmured Eliza. I looked at her. She was lost in her own thoughts, so I drifted into mine.

I had yearned for this sweet and rich candy, and here it was. I relaxed into the feeling of contentment. I gently stirred the candy in my mouth and discovered that the filling was smooth creamy marshmallow of a type I had never had before. It was light and not overly sweet. There was also a thin wafer at the base that melted quickly on my tongue. I wished I had more, and I knew then that I would buy them whenever I could.

My eyes turned toward the raised tram tracks that diminished in either direction in front of the goomey store. Their hard black lines focused my thoughts.

"Where do these tracks go?" I asked Eliza, between swallows.

"Downtown. It's the tram." Her voice was thick with marshmallow.

"Have you been on it? I want to ride it."

"A couple of times. It smells in there though."

"Did you go downtown?" I asked. But Eliza didn't answer. She was feeling around in her pocket, and then she walked over to the tracks and put a pfennig piece on one of the rails.

"Why did Eliza do that?" asked Quinn. I shrugged. We sat at the edge of the concrete embankment, waiting for the next tram to pass. The sky was bright blue, and the wind was blowing the clouds across the sky fast. My hair kept getting stuck in the marshmallow on my lips.

"Let's say that the horses are tied up at that tree, and when the tram comes, they spook and run off down the tracks," Eliza said.

"Okay. And then when we find them, we're too far from home to get back by nightfall, so we camp in Sebastian's Woods," I said. I had seen evidence of campers in the woods, like some trash and a campfire site and once even a torn shirt, and it had left me with an uneasy feeling at the time. I wanted Sebastian's Woods to be just for Eliza and me.

Suddenly, the tram crossing bell began to clang, and Quinn and August squealed with excitement. We rolled up our candy bags, and Eliza and I pulled the windblown hair from our sticky lips. The tram rumbled toward us, and there sat the shiny pfennig, awaiting its fate.

After the tram left and the noise died down, we found the pfennig in the dirt, only it was smooshed flat and hot. Eliza grabbed it and put it in her pocket, saying, "For my box," and then we pulled the boys up onto our backs and chased after our horses. They had spooked because of the tram and were disappearing, shimmering like mirages, in the haze down the tracks.

Out of the Woods

THERE IS NOTHING here. *The circle for the pony concession arena where I sit is dead, like the German cemetery. It feels scary. I can't even figure out if Stefan was real. I doubt everything, even his affection, and I feel woozy. I feel drunk. I get up and start back toward the woods.*

I stuff my stiff hands into my pockets, but it hardly staves off the cold. I yank out the cigarette pack and ditch it in the darkness of the forest floor, under the canopy of trees where the snow has not yet fallen. Enough of that. Then I stop.

I want something back. I cannot allow everything to be taken from me. I turn back to the pony arena and step across the threshold to the other side of the carnival world, behind the scenes. I can go there. I've been there before.

Stefan's trailer lights are off and all is silent. Maybe he and Jurgen and Mutti are asleep. Or maybe Stefan is lying awake thinking about me, remembering his lie. I know that even in darkness, his green eyes would glow, laced by long lashes. I know how his mouth would set, in regret, his lips a pout. He would cut his eyes to the side, trying to forget, but that would be impossible. Fine. Let him remember me always.

I turn toward the pony trailer. The big hinged doors are shut, but the ramp is in place so all I must do is muscle open the doors with minimal noise. I take my time because I have so much of it. I crack the door and a gust of wind does the work, opening it for me. Humid fragrant air spills out, green and warm and horsey. All the ponies' heads come up, and I can see the whites of their eyes, which roll in fear.

33

"Whoa, it's okay," I say, in an alto singsong. They know me, and they know what that means.

The heads dip down again, all but Kirsch's. She is watching for me as I approach. I have her bridle now. Gently I slip off her halter and she takes the bit. It never touches her teeth because I am so careful. I part the thick mane at the top of her head so that the bridle lies flat. Her fluff of white forelock falls over her forehead, protecting it. It's cold out there.

We have to back out to pass behind all the ponies' rumps. Kirsch raises her head to see behind herself, sliding her hooves alternately along the floorboards, cooperating as if she is eager to escape. I hold the reins and step forward, following her lead as if in a dance. I hear several murmuring nickers, and Kirsch's nostrils vibrate in answer, but she keeps backing. At the edge of the trailer, she turns and descends the ramp. Her white mane rises in the wind. I pull the doors closed and jump on. I let Kirsch take me into the woods.

She is warming me. I lean against her neck and lay my right arm along the length of it so that her mane covers my skin. My left arm lies downward, along her shoulder, feeling her steps. I lay my head along the crest of her neck, and the rhythm of her footfalls is soothing. My legs dangle.

She moves through the woods, and I look up now and then to see where we're headed. It's too dark and I don't know. I am dizzy, hot then cold. I push myself upright on Kirsch's back, and I see we are closer to the post apartments. I lie back down on Kirsch's neck, and she keeps walking until she decides to stop.

I cannot sit up. Kirsch lowers her head to the ground, and I slide off. I hit the ground, but it doesn't hurt. I look up and Kirsch turns to leave.

"No," I say. "Don't go."

But she goes. Her whiteness blends into the snow. A gust of wind brings a whoosh of white that lifts her mane and tail as she turns. I cannot see her anymore. She has become an invisible horse.

I stand up and my head pounds. I find myself at the entrance to an apartment building, its façade an expanse of concrete, broken by balconies. I pull open the heavy doors and go in. I climb one flight of stairs and ring the doorbell of the first door I see. But it's not the right door, I see that now, so I go up another flight of stairs and sense I am in the right place.

A door opens downstairs and then shuts.

I hear footsteps behind this door, the lock unbolting. I sag on the doorjamb. James opens the door, and I fall through the threshold onto the hardwood floor.

I have no idea how long I am out. Maybe a moment. Maybe an hour. I open my eyes. James looks at me with no expression. There are two Jameses, then one. He begins to look concerned. James is beside me on the floor. I roll onto my side and moan through a wave of nausea.

One James wipes my face with a cool cloth. One James does not move. I do not want to get up, and the blood is hammering in my head. Then both Jameses lift me onto the couch that is just like the one at my house. They cover me with a green army blanket that is just like the one at my house.

James leans close over me, kisses my forehead. His voice echoes, "You're burning up." I smell sugared coffee on his breath. I think of my mom.

Sebastian's Woods, 1969

"OKAY, LET'S SAY we have them now," I said.

Eliza and I were catching our breath after chasing Posey and Flyer down the tram tracks. We offloaded the twins, who ran ahead as we walked into the woods along a primitive trail padded by fallen leaves and crisscrossed by thick exposed roots. They kept their eyes on us over their shoulders, in case we veered off the path, and their hands kept busy shuttling goomeys from their little white bags into their little pink mouths.

"When I get my horse," I said, "I'm going to take overnight trail rides where you camp in hammocks with your horse tied up to a tree." Not that I had ever done anything remotely like that, but it sounded so romantic and essential, to sleep right next to your horse and listen to it breathe all night.

"My dad said I can get a horse when we move back to the States," Eliza said. She coughed, pulled a little bottle from her pocket, and swallowed some. "Cough medicine."

I wanted to say that my parents had said the same thing to me about a horse—because they had—but I was suddenly more concerned about when Eliza would be moving. Up until now, I hadn't even given a glimmer of a thought to our being separated. Eliza had become a part of me.

But that was real, that our dads would be reposted and we would be separated. It was only a matter of when.

We walked deeper into the woods, wordlessly heading toward a common destination. The boys slowed up to follow close behind. Days before, Eliza and I had found a secret place. It was a big fallen tree hidden in the woods, and we named it Sebastian. That was the most exotic name we could conjure. Sebastian the tree was another of our horses. The fallen tree was thick and straight, with a gentle slope toward the ground. One of us straddled it as if on horseback, and the other stood on the narrowest part and jumped up and down to make it vibrate like a plucked string. Sebastian would gallop or trot or even buck if you jumped just right. I could make Eliza laugh and fall off. You had to fall off sometime, gravity being what it is.

We had made our way to Sebastian and were sitting against him, side by side, fishing into our candy bags for goomeys. Eliza took a sip from her bottle of cough medicine. August was fetching fallen branches for Quinn, who was building a hideout. Then I realized that I did not want to eat any more goomeys, because my stomach hurt.

"When are you going back?" I asked.

"I don't know. It depends," she said.

"It depends." I had heard that saying before, from adults, but I could not make sense of it in any context. The way I looked at it, people said that instead of answering the question. I did not understand why Eliza would not want to answer my question, and I did not want to tell her that I did not know what she meant by "It depends."

Sometimes the way she acted—like she knew certain things— made it seem like she was a lot older than I was. Sometimes I felt really small, and I wondered when things would stop being so puzzling. I really looked up to Eliza, and even though I managed to keep pace with her, like when we were galloping through the woods, I was really just a moment behind, watching her movements, watching for what was next so I could follow.

I could not imagine her moving away. When you are an army kid, you get used to moving every two or three years or even more often. Making friends and then losing them becomes as normal as growing out of your favorite clothes.

But I had not kept any friends from when we lived in Hawaii or California. I did not know how to stay in touch once I had moved. Writing a letter seemed so abstract and impossible, even though my mom encouraged me and bought me pretty stationery that smelled like flowers. Anyway my friends never wrote back even when I tried. The girls I had been so close to sort of faded away into their own lives. But my bond with Eliza grew so fast in only a few months. It was different and more important, I was sure of it, and I already dreaded the thought of our parting.

"You ride, I'll jump," I said, trying to distract myself from thoughts of losing my friend. After Eliza found the right place to sit, where there were not any knobs or sharp places, I began to jump to make Sebastian trot.

"Can you spend the night tonight?" I said, breathing hard. Eliza was executing a perfect posting trot while I kept Sebastian's pace.

"I'll ask my dad," she said. But then she looked off into the distance, concentrating on something. I stopped jumping. "Wait. We have a family thing. I can't."

Eliza visited her mom at the hospital every single day, and sometimes the whole family met there. Most of the time she did not mention anything about the visits. But sometimes I could tell that she was worried, because she would not be as talkative or relaxed. I asked her pretty often how her mom was. She answered willingly but not in much detail. She would say that they ate lunch together or that her mom brushed her hair. Sometimes Eliza took the brush and did her mom's hair, and she even shampooed it sometimes.

Then one day I got the clue to stop asking.

"How was your mom yesterday?" I asked, open to hearing her tales.

"The same," Eliza said flatly, and her face turned to stone. "The same, the same, it's always the same, okay? Drop it."

I imagined that Eliza really missed her mother, and that thought sometimes made my chest hurt. I know her dad loved her and took good care of her, and I know her siblings wanted what was best for her, but there is no way to replace a mom. There just is not. Period.

We headed back toward home with the twins because we were all thirsty from candy and all that galloping around. Plus, since Eliza and I had taken the boys on an excursion, now I wanted some privacy with my best friend.

"Before I moved here, did you go to the goomey store a lot?" I asked. I wondered if Eliza had had another best friend in Munich who moved away, who maybe did not answer her letters, but I could not bring myself to ask the specific question. I did not really want any details about her life before I came into it.

"No. Before you came here, I didn't run around on horses all the time either," she said, and then she laughed over her shoulder. "Come on. Let's gallop on this trail and jump the roots."

We wildly whipped our horses' rumps with imaginary crops and egged them into a gallop. Swerving along the rough wooded trail, we jumped over exposed roots with perfect form.

In my mind's eye, I saw myself in harmony with the horse, leaning tight over its neck as it leaped, breaking the bonds of gravity.

"They'll be ready for their naps today," I said to Eliza as we pulled up to wait for the boys. Their little faces were red, and they whined to be picked up. So Eliza took August and I took Quinn, and we brought them home to my mom. She set down her pen and told us to run along.

Green Capes

I AM FEVER dreaming about something Eliza and I did a long time ago. I am struggling with the green blanket, because I am too hot. I cannot sleep. But I cannot bear to wake up either.

If I wake up, then my life goes back to normal, and it is too depressing to return to. I roll onto my side, with my face to the back of James's couch, and open my eyes to the dream. I am looking right into Eliza's blues, which somehow I see in full color in the darkness of the woods. We are each huddled beneath blankets we brought for our sleepover in Sebastian's Woods. The blankets are wool, scratchy green military issue, but at least they are warm.

"That wasn't comfortable," Eliza says. "What time do you think it is?"

"I don't know, but it must be morning. The sky is getting light."

"Let's move then. Let's walk until it's light, and then we can get something to eat at my house."

I make sure the fire is out. It is dead out. Then I bury Eliza's little bottle. I drank some last night. The cold weather made me cough, like Eliza coughs. She said it helps. I drank too much. My head spun. Eliza drank the rest.

We gather up two corners of our blankets and tie them around our necks so that we wear the green blankets like capes. But we cannot see the green yet. Everything is gray. We walk through the gray morning in the gray woods. Gray vapor forms before our faces. We walk until colors return and the day brightens.

"Come on. I want to show you something," says Eliza.

We keep going through the woods, but when we reach the edge, instead of following the tram tracks, we turn our horses across the tracks and walk along a busy road with a wide sidewalk.

The horses are not spooked by cars or traffic lights. They do not shy from the huge black pointy iron gates and the snarling stone gargoyles at the entrance to the old German cemetery either. I imagine our blankets draping the horses' hindquarters as we ride.

Eliza and I look at each other as we walk past the gates, as if daring each other to go in. But then an old couple wearing black coats, hats pulled low, walk toward the entrance, holding hands and looking serious. They have gotten out of a limousine with windows you cannot see into. Everything becomes quiet all of a sudden. Eliza takes my arm and says, "Come on."

And then she reins Posey through the gates and onto the crunchy gravel pathways of the German cemetery. Flyer follows, and I feel myself being swallowed up by the gloom of large dense trees that seem heavier and more ominous than those in Sebastian's Woods.

I have never been in a cemetery before—I have never had occasion to, and I am glad of it. I get a creepy feeling. I slow. But three strides in front of me goes Eliza as if she has walked the paths before and has a purpose for being here.

"Eliza, wait!" I say. My stomach is beginning to feel bad. I twist in the blanket, and I am trapped. "Can we sit down for a minute?"

I walk toward a concrete bench along the wide pathway, set back in a small alcove. Eliza and I sit down.

"What's wrong, Philippa? You look white!"

To avoid throwing up, I envision something soothing and beautiful, a white horse loping through clover up to its belly. I imagine its carefree life, galloping through the pasture to a large pond of fresh water. I begin to feel better and I come out of myself, begin looking around.

"This place is sort of creepy, don't you think?" I say. Large tombstones are mottled and stained from decades of rain and snow. Lichens and moss raise patterns along the edges, clinging to the rock for life.

"Creepy? No. I think it's sort of peaceful," she says. "I mean, it's so quiet. Listen. Even with the main road out there, just listen to the quiet."

I hold my breath. She is right. It is as if all the trees have absorbed the daily noise of the city beyond those pointy gates. But I am still uneasy. Before I try to make another argument for leaving, Eliza turns toward me.

"You might think I'm a freak, but I like to come here," she says. Her blue eyes look both confident and questioning.

I do not answer her right away because I sense she has more to say. But she stops, so I know it is my turn.

"I don't think you're a freak," I say. And I really don't.

"Sometimes I come here to think and be alone. It is a pretty solitary place," she says. "Even if there are other people here, they're all . . . alone. I mean, in a way, you know?"

"I guess I've never really thought about it," I say.

"I think about it a lot," she says.

Then we are quiet, and so is the cemetery. At the same moment, we untie our green blanket capes and let them drop to the bench.

"Look, it's not such a bad place," Eliza says, trying to convince me with her casual stance and arm gestures. She can tell I am doubtful. "There are winding pathways that we can gallop along—that is, as long as we don't make a huge ruckus. And sometimes the new flower arrangements are really beautiful."

"Yeah, I guess," I say, returning my gaze to the headstones, statues, bouquets, wreathes, and sprays of flowers. Some graves are better decorated than others, and I consider what it would take to evenly distribute the riches.

"Come on. I want to show you something—if you're feeling better," she says.

I stand. We run along the gravel pathways as if we are on bridle paths, cantering our horses past well-kept plots and headstones with thick wreathes and urns of fading flowers. The place is a labyrinth, and it is a wonder we find our way around. Except that, I realize, Eliza knows what she is doing.

I notice a building up ahead, aging and lichen covered, and Eliza leads me straight for it. The carved wooden doors are heavy, heavier than the one at the goomey store, and we both struggle to pull open just one of them. We go in. When the door closes behind us, it's like we've gone into a theater and the movie has already started. We are in the dark, but behind a plate-glass window that runs the length of the room are ten open caskets with lights shining on them, and inside of them are dead people.

We have entered a darkened theater of the dead. I walk steadily beside Eliza as she approaches the window, like a spooky horse staying close to a bold one. The cadavers smell like papier-mache gone bad. I have made papier-mache masks, so I know. But the faces look waxy, not like papier-mache. The flattened eyelids look like they are glued shut, like the glue is sort of seeping out.

I know for sure these people are dead even though it is the first time I have seen dead people. I just know.

The men are wearing suits with ties, and the women have on dresses that are freshly pressed and smooth. I cannot believe their hair is even done up nice. Everything is monotone gray and somber. Everyone's eyes are closed.

"Oh, man," I say. "Let's get out of here." I seriously am going to barf.

"Take it easy," says Eliza. She is transfixed, and she is calm. I look at her profile by turning my eyes without turning my head. I do not want her to know I am watching for her next move.

There is nobody else in the room, and I feel something building up inside of me. It is not fear, really. And it is not nausea. I am past that.

"Eliza, come on."

"Okay, but look—"

Then I realize I am holding my breath. The smell of death is so disgusting that I have quit breathing. I am suffocating. I snort out my nose, and I run out of the building into the cold, with Eliza right behind me. My chest is stinging inside and I am gulping the fresh air, and I run back to the bench in the alcove where the blankets are. I spin around to face Eliza.

"What the heck was that?" I yell, breathing heavily and pacing in front of the bench.

"I guess it's the mortuary. Or the morgue," she says. "I don't know."

"I mean, why did you take me in there? I don't want to go in there again!"

"Okay. Well, I thought—"

"Well, you thought wrong!"

Eliza sits down on the bench and looks at her hands. I keep walking around, feeling the need to burn off some noxious chemical in my bloodstream. I feel hot and then cold, and then I realize it was panic.

"Okay, look Eliza, I'm sorry," I say. I reach for my blanket and retie it into a cape.

She looks up. "Maybe I went too far. You're not ready for that place."

Not ready? Here she is again, one step ahead of me, like I am not grown up enough to tour a dead zone.

"Oh, come on," I say. "You have to admit it. That place is gross!"

Neither one of us says anything for a few minutes, long enough for our breathing to slow, for me to cool off.

I wonder why Eliza is so intrigued by death, and suddenly I feel shame. But I have no words for the rush of thoughts and feelings. I retreat, softening my voice.

"How did you find it?" I ask.

"I wandered in one day," she says, reaching for her blanket, adopting my casual tone. Then she says mischievously, "I go every now and then, you know, to stay current."

Eliza has a way of cracking me up, and before I know it Flyer begins hopping around and pulls to gallop out of the alcove, with my cape flying behind. Eliza laughs too and jumps to her feet, and then we gallop back toward the pointy gates and into the real world, the real noisy moving world full of color outside the cemetery.

I straighten my legs on James's couch, I am running, and I twist under the blanket. I still will not open my eyes.

The Midway, 1969

"I WANT TO ride the horses and run run run like the cowboys," said Quinn. His face was turned upward as we walked toward the Little Oktoberfest carnival along the wooded path. His shoulders had squinched up around his ears and his little feet began to do a jig, almost like he wanted to trot right out of his skin.

"Okay, run like the cowboys," I said. "What about you, August? Are you ready to run too?"

"I don't want to run. I don't want to go. Will you stay with me?"

"I'll go right along with you. Don't worry," I said, and he tightened his grip on my hand. "You guys are going to love this, I promise. These ponies are just your size, with saddles just your size. You'll be cowboys alright. Come on, let's trot!"

We began to jog along the last section of the trail through the trees, and the path was narrow and twisty but hard-trodden and smooth enough so you would not trip over anything. Sometimes I had to duck to avoid branches, so I swooped down to one side, imagining the long dark mane of my horse's neck right by my ear.

Finally we had to slow down and stop to catch our breath. The boys took in huge gulps of air and their cheeks blew up like pink balloons on either side of their faces.

"Look! A Ferris wheel!" said August, his fear emptying at the clearing, where we surveyed the transformation that had taken place in the usually vacant field. Lights were strung everywhere, giving the carnival a glittering excitement that quickened my breath again and

45

lured the twins away from me. I followed them closely onto the midway, where you could step up to booths, hand over coins, and try your hand at winning cheap stuffed animals and trinkets. Everything seemed shiny and bright, so colorful I wanted to reach for it all.

The whole place was a merry-go-round of smells, first burgers, then beer, then pretzels, then wurst. First I felt hungry and then disgusted, and then I felt hungry again. The music changed with each booth we passed too. I scanned the grounds for the pony concession that Eliza had told me about. She was right. It was there, at the end of the midway. I could see the round arena encircled by tiny lights.

"Look over here, guys. Let's go see the ponies."

"I want a pretzel," said Quinn, who must have caught a whiff of their warm yeasty fragrance. I noticed a boy with a pretzel on a ribbon looped around his neck.

"Me too! Philippa, can we get pretzels?" said August. As we walked toward the concession, I counted out the right amount of money in U.S. coins, because the Oktoberfest traded in dollars.

"Point to the one you want," I told the boys, who chose the biggest ones they could see, and then I set the ribbons around their necks to secure the pretzels in case they ever let go. They held the oversized pretzels up to their faces, and it looked like they had on masks, but I could see their eyes and smiling mouths.

"Give me a taste, each of you. Pay your toll to the troll!" And they pulled a small section from the fresh soft pretzels for me to sample. *Mmmm.* Yummy, hot, and salty.

"Let's go riding," I said, as we strolled toward the ponies. Both Quinn and August were busy with their pretzels so I slowly herded them in the direction of the arena.

I stepped up to the ticket booth, where a big woman sat, taking money and doling out little red tickets. She had fat fingers and frizzy red hair, and she did not smile, so I kept my eyes on my hands and the money. I put out the right amount for two rides, and she pushed two tickets toward me. Her rings pinched her skin below the knuckles so that her fingers resembled jumpy little wursts.

Then the boys and I waited a few minutes, watching the ponies until they were done with the session. Around they went, along the perimeter of the arena. In the center stood the ringmaster, a tall teenage German boy with a whip in one hand and a cigarette in the other. He had greasy hair and a greasy forehead, and he wore tall black boots. Every now and then, he cracked the whip for effect, but it did not scare the ponies or make them trot. They continued around the metal rail at a walk, and the twins and I leaned into the cold rails to watch.

"I want that one," said Quinn, pointing to a furry black pony near the front of the line.

"Okay, but you might not get to ride that one," I said. "We can try, though. Here are your tickets. Can you guys hold them? Then you can give them to that guy when you ride, okay?"

The tickets became moist little origami in their fists.

"Okay, it's our turn," I said, and we filed into the arena with several other children and their parents. Quinn's pony was unoccupied, so we went immediately to it.

"Pet your pony first," I said, "and tell him you're going to ride."

Quinn gave the pony one pat on the shoulder and then began tugging at whatever he could reach, the stirrup, the cinch leather, to pull himself up. I hoisted him up onto the pony, positioned his legs comfortably, and set his hands on the saddle horn. "Hold on. We're going to get a pony for August."

Ponies behind and in front of Quinn's were already taken, so August and I walked to the end of the line, where a small skinny brown pony stood, with its head down. I hoped August would not notice that he had gotten the most pathetic pony, the one rejected by everyone. Instead he gently stroked its nose and then asked me to put him on the pony. Meanwhile the ringmaster was going to each mounted child, taking the tickets, and stuffing them into the front pocket of his tight pants. I got out of the arena before the ringmaster took the ticket from August.

The ringmaster walked back to the center of the arena, taking long deliberate strides, and his tall shiny black boots made a spectacle of themselves in the sawdust arena. He lifted the whip and twirled it in such a way that when he flicked his wrist, bringing the whip down, it cracked loudly in the air, making me jump. The ponies waited a moment, unfazed, and then walked on.

Quinn was smiling, clamped tightly to the saddle horn by way of his grip. August was tight on too, but I was sure he was going to cry. The ponies circled for the longest time, it seemed, but that was probably because I felt what each of the twins felt, in alternating waves that swept over me. There was the ecstasy of being on horseback that Quinn felt, the gentle rhythm of the horse's motion that he easily followed, the swirling activity of the carnival beyond the bright lights of the arena. Then there was the fear that August experienced, his body stiff and jolting, the feeling of no control, the unfamiliar gait of a four-legged beast that no amount of Horsey-playing could teach.

I had to look away from him so that he could face his fear on his own. I did not want my expression—whatever it might look like to him—to make him think he should be afraid. I knew he would be safe on the pony just walking around the ring.

I glanced over at the woman in the ticket booth. She was counting money. Then I noticed another teenage boy with features similar to the ringmaster's, wide-set eyes, messy brown hair, and broad bony shoulders. This boy was my age, and even from across the arena I could tell his eyes were green. He looked busy, carrying a pitchfork and bucket, heading behind the arena to where the horses were kept. Unconsciously I kept my eyes on him as I imagined what it must be like behind the scenes. I wondered where the horses stayed when they were not in the ring. I fantasized about going back there and brushing them. Before I could look away, though, the boy met my eyes and smiled at me. Did he notice I was staring?

I turned back to the arena with a red-hot face and saw the ringmaster take one last deep drag from his cigarette, flick it into the dirt, and leave it there, smoldering. He lowered his whip.

"Ohhh," he said.

Not "Whoa" but "Ohhh," with his lips in a tight O shape. The ponies stopped so immediately that the entire row of little riders' bodies was swept forward and then righted. I had to smile because it reminded me of silly comedy routines when all the characters, hurrying in one direction, have a pileup. I was relieved to have something to hook my attention to in case that German boy was still looking at me.

As I went toward the gate to the arena, I noticed the twins had exchanged moods. Now August was smiling and relieved, and Quinn was cross. His body felt like a slab of stone when I pulled him from the black pony, with gentle encouragement that he would get to ride again soon. August was supple as a goomey snake, beginning to slither down before I even got to him. Then, even though he had been terrified when he was astride, he hugged the brown pony's neck and said, "Thank you."

The boys each grabbed one of my hands, and we walked out of the arena. I hated leaving the ponies. Another group of kids was filing in to jump up on their backs for another go-round, and I thought, *This is what the ponies do all day—tolerate a revolving bunch of kids getting on and off, on and off?* I was so busy thinking about the ponies' plight, my eyes studying the dirt and sawdust, that I plowed right into the German boy with the green eyes. His bucket of water sloshed onto the ground by my feet, and the boys jumped out of the way.

"Sorry," he said, and he leaned down to place the bucket on the ground. Then he stood straight up and looked right into my eyes. I was glad I had the twins' hands to anchor me. I was expecting something to happen.

"Philippa, come on," said Quinn.

"Okay, yeah," I said. "Hold on." Then I said to the German boy, "Sorry. We have to get going..."

"Wait," the boy said, and he walked a few strides to the ticket booth. He said something to the woman in the booth, but she did not answer. Then he came back with two little red tickets for the boys.

"Come ride again," he said and extended the tickets.

"Okay," I said. *"Danke."* Quinn and August reached for the tickets, but I held them up, just out of their reach, and looked away, off into the midway. I was planning my next visit to Little Oktoberfest.

Pointy Gates

ELIZA AND I run back into Sebastian's Woods, away from the German cemetery and toward the goomey store. Our green blanket capes flow behind us. Maybe it is too early and the store is closed.

"Think Frau Jaw is open?" I say.

I try the heavy door, and sure enough, we go in.

Spurlos the rat dog begins to bark his head off. The goomey lady comes through the door from her back room right away but with unusual clumsiness, pulling on her sweater and accidentally pushing the door farther ajar than usual. I see into the room. It is golden and warm compared with the stark white brightness of the store. I smell cooking. I see a bureau, a mirror. I see the end of a bed, with rumpled sheets. The sheets move; there is someone in the bed. The dog does not stop yapping.

"Spurlos!" yells the goomey lady, and he cowers where he stands. The goomey lady's eyes look puffy as she turns her attention to us. Her lips are thickly smeared with pink. I know we are trying her patience.

Eliza and I choose our candy quickly, calculate our sums, pay with exact change.

"Danke," we say in unison to the towering figure behind the glass case.

I make it to the door first, and I shove it with my hip and turn the stubborn knob at the same time. We run into the cold and gallop up the embankment.

"Did you see that?" I scream.

"It was a foot!" says Eliza. We climb out of the gulley and up onto the road.

"It was a man's foot," I say, breathless. "With probably a whole man attached!"

"And her dress was unbuttoned!" Eliza says. "Frau Jaw was buttoning her dress!"

Our blood races through our brains. We gallop home, sucking in the cold air, our green capes a blur. I begin to feel overheated and sweaty. On my way up the curving staircase, I twist out of the scratchy blanket. But I can still feel it behind me, where I am lying, on James's couch, with a hammering in my head.

I remember Eliza dumping out the contents of our white bags on the wooden floor of my bedroom upstairs. I have no red goomeys, but I know I can trade some of my greens and yellows to Eliza.

"Do you think that's her boyfriend?" I say, trying to fire up the subject of the goomey lady and the mysterious man on the bed.

"Or maybe just her husband," Eliza says.

"The goomey lady is married?" I say, incredulous. "No way!"

"Well, she's not Fraulein Jaw."

"True. They were in bed together, though," I say, trying to get a good story going. But Eliza has lost interest in the subject, as if in her own mind she has already taken it to the end and there is nothing left for two 13-year-olds to discuss.

"We interrupted them, for sure..." I continue.

I want to turn the subject around and around and look at it from all angles and even make up stuff. But Eliza will not budge. She sits concentrating on her goomeys and lining them up according to color and kind.

Now I have lost interest too and begin to sulk, standing outside the wall Eliza has erected around herself. My mom calls from downstairs to see if we are ready to go downtown to buy coats. I jump up at the opportunity, and Eliza goes to call her dad and tell him that we are headed out as planned.

Eliza needs a new winter coat too, and my mom has offered to take her shopping with us. We persuade my mom to take the tram instead of the car, and we show her where the nearest stop is, not far from the goomey store. But we do not point out the store for fear she would forbid us from going.

51

"How often does the tram come by here?" asks my mom. She is standing close to the tracks and leaning out to see as far down them as she can.

"About every twenty minutes," says Eliza. "You never have to wait long."

"Do you use the tram a lot, Eliza?" says my mom.

"No, but it makes it easier to get downtown."

My mom and Eliza keep up a light conversation, and I just get madder at Eliza. She thinks she knows more than I do about the man in Frau Jaw's bed. And then she will not talk to me about it. Plus she will not talk to me about her mom. I know that she knows more than she will say—about a lot of things. For the first time ever I weigh the possibility that maybe we are not such good friends after all.

I tune back in to Eliza and my mom's conversation, but it is going along the same superficial lines. Eliza makes my mom laugh. Finally the tram comes down the tracks, alternately rumbling and screeching, and we get on.

Eliza is right about one thing. It does smell in there. It smells of too many people, spicy and humid, and I wish the windows would open or the door would stay ajar so that the place could air out. A closed smelly place is all my stomach needs to feel bad. It brings back memories of that gross morgue with its one-of-a-kind stench. I remind myself to breathe.

I move down the aisle and notice that no one makes eye contact. There are no kids my age, just worn-out old women and men, it seems. They look out the window, but they are not seeing anything. They seem like zombies.

I sit down on a bench next to the window on the left side of the tram, and Eliza slides in next to me. The tram starts up, grinding sort of, not smooth at all. My mom stands in the aisle right next to Eliza, holding tight to a rail, swaying with the motion. It seems that in a way my mom has adopted Eliza as one of her own. Just because Eliza's mom is dying does not mean she can have mine. I freeze at that thought and try to dismiss it. I cannot believe I thought that. The tram is picking up speed.

"Look, Eliza," I say over the clatter and chug of the tram. "There's your favorite place." We are passing the pointy gates of the German cemetery.

"Oooh-eee-oooh," I say, in a mock scary tone, but Eliza keeps a stone face.

My mom bends down and leans toward the window to see what I am referring to. When she sees the gates glide by, she stands up and looks at me with an expression that tells me at once that I have gone over the line. But lucky for me, she says nothing, and we three ride along in silence for another interminable time before we get to our stop downtown.

"This is it," says Eliza, and she stands up quickly, weaves past my mom, and leads us toward the door. I bite my lip as I walk past my mom. She is staring at me and I have to look at her.

"What's going on?" she loud-whispers.

"Nothing," I loud-whisper back. And then I tell myself to hold to it. To enter another world when I exit the tram, a world in which I will behave myself even if I do not understand Eliza. A world in which I will be a good friend to her. I step out into the fresh cold air of downtown Munich.

"Which way is it?" I ask, looking directly into Eliza's eyes. She matches my stare, tips her head, and says, "Right this way!" Then we link arms and stride off, and my mom can barely keep up.

The Ponies, 1969

ELIZA WAS UNUSUALLY quiet today, and I knew she was thinking about her mom. It was not anything she ever discussed with me, so I had to let her have her space for her own private thoughts. When she was ready to open up, I could be there for her.

School was well under way, but we did not have classes together so we saw each other only at lunch and recess. Most of the time, we walked to school together too. I walked alone from my house, through a section of duplexes, and out to the playing fields, where there was a hill for sledding. Eliza's house was right behind it, and she would appear at the top and come running down, sometimes acting as if she were out of control, with arms flailing, to make me laugh. Then we went through a section of woods behind the hospital. Sometimes we went through the hospital, sometimes around, depending on our mood. School was across the street from the hospital.

Of course Eliza included me in her friendships at school, so that made everything easier. I was past my most nervous time and had become accustomed to the school week. It finally dawned on me that I was not the only one in a totally new situation. I always forgot that. But now I was beginning to like school again.

And I could not believe my luck at having a carnival a short gallop away. It would be here for only a few weeks, though. Eliza and I went to the Little Oktoberfest almost every day after school and on the weekends.

We spent a lot of our money on the shotgun concession halfway down the midway. I was a good shot, and for my winnings I chose the feather whips. That is what I called them. The feather whip resembled a feather duster, only with a thin, reedy handle. The feathers came in all the beautiful colors—bright lime green and goomey-lady lipstick pink and turquoise blue and, of course, purple—and were bunched together at the tip. So it was a sort of combination magic wand and whip, and I began to carry one around all the time, my color choice corresponding to my mood each day.

The feather whip was better than an imaginary one for urging Flyer on if she balked at an obstacle or spooked at something scary. I had a bunch of feather whips at home already, stuffed into a magnum champagne bottle. Today the orange one was tucked into the back pocket of my cords, so that it bobbed along behind me as I walked.

"If we hang around long enough, maybe we'll get to brush the ponies," I told Eliza, remembering my fantasy the day I had taken the boys to ride and ran into the German boy with the green eyes. "Don't you want to?"

We had finished our burgers and were starting on our caramel apples when Eliza finally began to perk up. I really wanted to go to the ponies, but it wasn't happening. Instead I followed Eliza's lead and we ambled around the fairgrounds, watching the carnies do their thing. They yelled in English, with heavy German accents, and they looked at us right in the eye and tried to draw us in. I walked close to Eliza because she had already done all this before.

"It's all the same as last year," Eliza said. We stood at the foot of the huge twirling swing ride with a name I never tried to pronounce. "But this one's the best. Let's go on it."

I jumped at the chance to do anything to cheer up Eliza. We bought our tickets, found two swings next to each other in the circle, and fastened the chains across our laps. I quit eating my apple in anticipation of the ride and clutched it in my hand along with my feather whip.

Then slowly the top part of the ride began to revolve and it picked up speed so that the circle of swings went around like a merry-go-round. I looked over my shoulder at Eliza, and she was perched as expectantly as I was. Pretty soon we were traveling so fast that our swings pulled out from the ground and we were lifted above the carnival, feeling the pull of centrifugal force and the cold late-afternoon wind on our cheeks. I loved it! I realized that I had a huge smile on my face as the world around me flashed by in a kaleidoscope of colors and lights. Holding the swing chains tight in my fists, I leaned my head back and looked behind me, at Eliza upside down, and she screamed, "Hang on!" Then we both screamed together, and righting myself, I had to gasp to catch my breath. And I realized that for the first time I was in front of Eliza.

When the ride slowed down and finally stopped, we staggered down the ramp, our bodies close, like drunkards, and headed in the direction of the pony concession. My caramel apple was glued to my mitten. Eliza had the same situation going, and we thought it was the funniest thing. I was doubly happy to see Eliza laugh. I stuffed my feather whip back into my pocket, and we pulled ourselves together as we neared the pony ride, because the ponies were in the middle of a session and we didn't want to spook them. We watched them go round and round, and I regretted that I was too big to ride them. That would have looked ridiculous.

Eliza and I leaned against the cold metal railing, watching the ponies. The ringmaster boy stood in the center of the ring cracking the whip, looking important, and ignoring us. The younger boy, who was probably 15, noticed Eliza and me, but I looked away real fast. Besides, he was always busy, moving about with purpose. The ticket lady sat in her cramped booth under a bright light, and I realized it made her look like a mean fortune-teller.

"Let's go around back," said Eliza. "Come on. I'll show you."

I followed her, stepping over wires and hoses and odd pieces of lumber. "Have you been back here before?" I said. I was nearly breathless.

"Once."

Behind the arena stood a trailer where the family lived and also a big long truck trailer for stabling and traveling with the ponies. I had never been behind the scenes at a carnival, and my bubble was burst. I wanted it to be magical in some way, sparkly, organized for fun and pleasure, but it looked like any old trailer park. I noticed that the trailer where the family lived wasn't quite level. It gave me a dizzy feeling. The ponies' trailer looked level and sturdy, though, and I was glad of it.

When the ponies were not working in the arena, they stood in the trailer crosswise, stacked up like Oreos. A big silver-white pony was in the far back of the trailer, munching hay, and there were a couple of small ponies in there too. But the others were in the arena. So Eliza and I walked up the ramp and into the trailer, where it was warm and quiet. The ponies turned from their hay to look at us, and after pocketing our mittens we bit off pieces from our caramel apples and fed them from our palms.

"This little black one is drooling all over the place," Eliza said. Her hands were slick and shiny. "I think he likes it!"

"I'm giving mine to this cob," I said. I didn't have an appetite for my apple anymore anyway because it was much more fun to feed it to the ponies. Their muzzles were so wiggly and sensitive and easily knew the difference between, say, a finger and a carrot, or the skin of your hand and the skin of an apple. And when they gently took the treat and pulled it into their warm mouths, they exhaled such nice-smelling humid breath. The trailer was already filled with that warm horse-breath smell, and now there was a tang of apple in the air too.

"Okay, it's all gone," Eliza was saying to the persistent ponies. "Really! Frisk me if you want. Okay, see?"

Then she turned around in mock seriousness, with her arms extended. "Check my back pockets too. Go ahead."

The black and blond ponies were rubbing her all over with their nosy noses. Eliza and I laughed, and I stood by the white pony, who was letting me hold her head in my arms and seemed to be dozing off.

And then we were startled by a German voice. *"Was machen Sie?"*

It was the boy with the green eyes, standing outside the trailer and peering in at us. Eliza and I just stared at the horse slobber on our hands, unable to answer the question. I felt like a trespasser.

Finally I remembered some German, for "apple" and "horses." *"Apfel. Die Pferde,"* I stammered. In my panic, I had forgotten that the boy had spoken English to me earlier.

The boy smiled and nodded and pointed to a bucket of brushes. Then he turned around, and we could hear him walking back to the arena. We went into a frenzy of action.

"Let's do the big one first," I said, but Eliza wanted to brush the small blond pony.

"Look! I can even brush down his other side from here—he's so tiny!" she said.

The ponies stood perfectly still for their grooming, as if they did not want it to end. The silver-white mare lifted her chin and twisted her muzzle slightly when I got into a rhythm while brushing her neck. When I looked closely at her coat I could see all different colored hairs that made up her silver-white coat, even black ones. That was amazing to me, that all those colors made white. Her mane was made up of silver, white, beige, and black hairs, and I pulled out a small clump—it didn't hurt her—and wound it up like a little white lariat. I put it deep in my pocket so she would always be near me.

We braided the ponies' forelocks as a finishing touch, giggling, because they looked so cute with their hairdos.

Earlier than I expected the arena ponies came walking in a line toward the trailer barn. Both of the German boys came along, and then I saw the mother as she lumbered with the metal box of money toward her tilted trailer, walking wide semicircles around the piles of manure. Without even exchanging words with the boys, Eliza and I helped take off the saddles and curry the ponies' backs and undersides, where the saddle and girth pushed their fur down flat. We picked up all their little hooves to clear them of stones and manure. I saw the older boy scowl at the younger one and then turn and leave.

The ponies stood untied. I wondered why they did not want to run off into the night. They closed their eyes and ground their teeth and swished their tails. Then the younger boy sent them into the trailer, up the plank in a certain order that they already knew, and they lined up crosswise, sometimes nipping at one another but mostly getting along fine. I climbed up the ramp and checked to make sure each pony had a bunch of hay to eat.

Once they were settled in, the boy looked at me and asked, *"Wie heisst du?"*

I moved closer to one of the ponies and hugged its neck. I was so embarrassed. With my nose in its mane I said, "Philippa Swift."

"Ja?" he said. Then he looked at Eliza and said her name as if it were a question.

"Ja," she said. He was smiling, almost laughing at us, it seemed. I realized then that Eliza already knew this boy. I tried to ignore the weird feeling I had at Eliza for not telling me. He said his name was Stefan, and then he named off all the ponies. I could not concentrate on the names, but I caught the one for the white cob, Kirsch, way in the back.

I found myself unable to make eye contact with Eliza, so I just stared at Kirsch. I liked her the best because she was my size. She did not work in the ring with the other ponies. She was old—I could tell by the way her long teeth stuck out—and now she was retired. Stefan knew I liked her.

Then I wondered why Eliza had not ever told me that she already knew this German boy. After all, hadn't we discussed Oktoberfest, and hadn't we obsessed over horses since the moment we met, in the clover behind my house?

Stefan grabbed up his bucket and turned to leave, and I finally faced Eliza. But I could not say it. I could not say, "Why didn't you tell me you knew him?" I could not say, "Why do you keep these secrets from me?" And I could not make sense of my feelings. Was I angry or hurt? And why did my heart seem to bleed out warm blood into my guts every time I saw Stefan?

I turned away from Eliza and noticed Stefan and his brother standing by the trailer house. Eliza saw too. I could barely hear the brother say something to Stefan. I could tell it was about Eliza and me. Then I heard the brother say "Mutter." He threw down his cigarette like a dart and smooshed it with his big black boot. Then Stefan looked at me, but he didn't smile.

"Stefan loves you," Eliza sang to me, teasingly. She swallowed some medicine. Then she laughed, kind of mean. It was almost a cackle.

"He does not." To get her back, I added, "His brother loves you." But my stomach clenched up.

Moonbeams

I AM READY for bed, but I am not under my soft feather blanket. I am still on James's couch. I want to be in my bed. Everything smells different. I almost wake up, but I cannot. I want to stay under.

I remember my mom coming into my room to tuck me in. She sits on the edge of my bed, with an anxious look, and I can tell she wants to talk about something.

"Philippa, do you and Eliza talk about her mother?" she asks.

"No. Not lately," I say. "She doesn't bring it up, and I don't really know what to say, I mean, how to say what I mean. Whatever that is."

"There's really not a lot you can say. There's not much anyone can do. Except you can be a good friend to Eliza."

"She's my best friend ever, Mom. I feel sorry for her that she doesn't live with her mom."

"Yes, but she has a good daddy and a good family that help take care of her," she says.

"It's not the same," I say.

"That's true," she says, and she stands up and walks toward the window, with her hands on her hips, arching and stretching to loosen her back. "Let's open your curtains. You'll get moonbeams tonight."

Moonbeams are my mom's invention, something magical, mystical. As long as I can remember she has created such realities to distract me from worldly worries. And even the recent moon landing itself did nothing to lessen the mysterious quality of the moon in my mind. She explained the phases, the waning and the waxing. She told me about how the new moon isn't visible to us. I used to believe everything she told me. But now I reserve the right to disbelieve.

"Mom," I say. I'm unconvinced. "Moonbeams?" I cannot decide if I should encourage her or shut her down. I concentrate on the warmth of my feather blanket, how lightly it rests on my body and how the feathers radiate my body heat back to me.

"Oh, yes. Moonbeams are a gathering of silver from heaven—a blessing for all children," she says, reminding me of the fable she has invented. "In fact, moonbeams are the blue-white children of sunshine. You're my moonbeam."

Then she walks back across the wooden floor to my bed and sits down again. I feel safe when she comes near. I keep quiet, waiting for her to fill in the silence with something I can grab hold of.

"Here, let's bolster your pillow like this now," she says. The pillow feels fatter. "See how your cheek glows? Now, close your eyes and feel the moonbeams, and reflect them back toward me. Feel good?"

"Yes," I say. And I focus on the feeling of moonbeams on my face, imagining a silver smile on my lips, like the outline of a crescent. I relax and my eyelids flutter open. "Mom?" I see the whites of her eyes, like slivers of moons themselves. When she looks at me, I see unwavering love.

"What, baby?"

"What happens when we die?" I watch for her gaze to falter, but she looks at me steadily and then she passes her hand gently along the side of my face.

"We go to heaven so that we can look down on those we love, and watch after them," she says.

I have heard that story from her before, and I want to hear something different, something more compelling that I can believe. Can that really be all? How can we know? How can Eliza live each day with only that?

"So when Eliza's mom dies, she'll be up by the moon?" I ask, stretching the story, hoping it will break so that she can tell me a newer, better one.

"Oh, Philippa. Don't get ahead of yourself. Eliza's mom is not going to die."

"Yes, she is, Mom. You know she is. Everybody knows. Why can't people just say so?"

Then she loses her composure. Why won't she tell me something *real? She slumps down, and the tone of her voice gets lower too: "I don't know." There. Finally. "Dying is hard to grasp. It defies our understanding. It becomes an unspoken reality."*

"But I need to say it," I say, sitting upright. "I need to understand it."

She eases me back onto my pillow and holds my face in her hands. They are cool.

"As soon as you understand it," she says, "would you please explain it to me?"

Then she kisses me gently on the lips, and I smell sugared coffee on her breath.

"Now go to sleep," she says, and she fades from the room. I turn my gaze to the window, toward the moon. It is on the wane, and it peers back at me, as if it knows everything but isn't telling.

The Kiss, 1969

LITTLE OKTOBERFEST WAS scheduled to leave on Monday, so on Saturday evening Stefan took Kirsch out of the trailer for me. She glowed in the twilight, and I brushed her as she browsed along the edge of the clearing.

Eliza had had to go home early, and her mood had been so low that nothing I did or said seemed to make her feel better, and believe me, I tried. I won three feather whips at the shotgun concession, and I let her choose the colors. She chose purple, orange, and green, and I told her that they were all for her. At least I got a smile from her. She stuffed them in her back pocket, and I watched her walk toward home. The bright colors of the feather whips, as they bounced with her walk, belied her misery.

"Kirsch ist so gross und schön," I said to Stefan as I brushed the cob's silver mane. I had said she was big and beautiful. Kirsch was really big only compared to the ponies, but she was beautiful for sure.

I was trying my German to take my mind off of Eliza. And as long as I spoke German, so did Stefan.

"Willst du reiten?" Stefan asked, inviting me to ride. Maybe he could tell I felt out of sorts and he wanted to cheer me up.

"Ja," I said, quickly, so the chance wouldn't get away. Stefan gestured for me to take the lead line, and he took the whip. Stefan had such a polite manner, and he made me feel comfortable. We walked side by side to the arena, but our shoulders never touched.

It seemed unbelievable to me that I was going to ride Kirsch. There

63

was no one around. Mutter had closed the ticket booth and shut off the big overhead light. But the arena was lit by little white bulbs strung all along the roofline.

I brought Kirsch into the ring, and Stefan gave me a leg up by cupping his hands around my bent left knee and hoisting me up as I swung my right leg over. My new purple maxi coat, by way of the deep slit in the back, fell easily into place on either side of Kirsch. Her back was plump and padded with her thick coat, not hard like Sebastian's. My legs stretched when I hugged her with them, and when Stefan backed into the center of the ring, Kirsch started walking along the railing. She knew what to do. I had no reins to hold so I twisted my fingers into her silver-white mane, and then I let fly a few pieces of hay that had somehow braided themselves in.

I wished Eliza were there to see me. To make her envious? Or so that she could ride too and everything would be better? I didn't know how I felt; I felt both ways.

Kirsch was frisky. Stefan raised the whip and she went into a smooth trot. She lowered her head and snorted out her nose, and we trotted around the arena until I could feel her warm up beneath me. I felt like I could ride her all night. She had a smooth, even trot, and her head swayed gently left and right as she stepped along.

Then Stefan raised the whip again, and Kirsch broke into a canter, leaning into the curve of the ring. I held the mane until I got the rhythm, and I tried to focus ahead, between her ears, like sighting the shotgun at the shooting concession. But then she lowered her head, relaxing, and it all blended, the railing, the lights, the railing, the lights, dizzying, so I moved my eyes along her mane and down to my hands. I felt like I was in heaven, like I was where I belonged. I caught her stride, released the silver-white mane, and brought my hands straight out to my sides. They flapped like wings, just small easy wingbeats. *I could be a circus rider,* I thought. *I could stand up on Kirsch's back right now and do an arabesque.*

Around and around we went. It was slow motion, easy, and I could hear nothing but Kirsch's gentle snorts that matched the rhythm of the canter—one two three, one two three, *eins zwei drei.* Then I was breathing hard, and Kirsch was warmer. Stefan lowered the whip, and Kirsch came down to a walk. She tucked her chin and swished her tail. Then she blew her nose loud, and Stefan and I smiled at each other.

We let her walk around the circle a couple of times until she cooled down. I leaned forward along her neck and hugged it, breathing her in, and then I leaned all the way back so that my head gently bounced with the motion of her rump. For a few long moments, I totally forgot about Stefan in the center of the ring. Finally Stefan whoaed Kirsch, and I got off and led her back to the trailer. While I brushed her, Stefan fetched a bucket of fresh water.

"*Ganz gut, ja?*" he said.

"*Ja,*" I said. This was good. I was so happy and relaxed. Then I led Kirsch up the ramp. We squeezed between the trailer wall and the ponies' rumps to get to the back of the trailer, and the ponies tightened their tails against their bodies to make room. I tied up Kirsch's lead line and hugged her, burying my nose in her fragrant mane.

Then Stefan came up behind me, quietly, expectantly, it seemed, and I felt him standing too close. It didn't feel right, so I ducked under Kirsch's neck to get away and pushed between her and the next pony, and then I walked along the rumps to the ramp of the trailer. My stomach clenched up, and I sucked in the cold air and let my eyes adjust to the darkness.

For a moment I stood at the edge of the trailer. As if I could see behind myself like a horse does, I envisioned Stefan standing at the back of the trailer with Kirsch. And then I kept walking, down the ramp and away from the trailer and the carnival, away from the warmth and smell of the horses, toward the playground that stood in a clearing, lit up by the moon. It was full.

I shivered as I sat down on a swing and took its two cold chains in my hands. Why did I feel so scared? Riding Kirsch was the best, but Stefan had ruined it. I loved Kirsch. I didn't love Stefan. And now here he was; he had followed me. I saw him come out of the dark into the clearing. He kept coming and he was smiling, but the way he walked looked so serious. I shivered again, and he came up close, drawing in near me. I awkwardly let him closer by opening my legs. I should not have done that. He put his hands around me, into my coat, next to my body. He was warm.

"*Hast du angst?*" he asked.

I thought he asked if I was hungry. Why would he ask that? I wasn't hungry. But anyway, the only answer I had was no. I said, "Nein," but then he kissed me. His lips opened just a little bit, and inside was a big dark world that I almost fell into, but I did not want to go. I wondered when it would be over so I could go home. I wanted to cry and I felt it welling up inside, and when I shivered he pulled his lips away and held me closer.

I held my breath. Finally he let go, stood back, and looked at me. I got off the swing and said bye and turned away toward home.

I started off running slowly, along the same path I had taken with the twins, breathing hard because I had held my breath for so long. But then I got skittish in the dark, so I hurried out of the woods and tried to stay in the pools of lamplight, and then I was running on the fastest horse, leaning forward on its neck, sucking in the cold night air.

When I finally got to my house, I turned the key in the door and ran upstairs to my room. I fell on my bed, silently crying, trying to block everything out—it was too much—and I cried myself to sleep. In the morning, I was under my feather blanket, and I vaguely remembered the night before, my mom quietly pulling off my shoes, my grubby cords, and purple maxi, and tucking me into bed.

Snow Angel

I AM GALLOPING along the gravel path of the German cemetery. My legs jerk as I lie on James's couch like a dog's when it runs in its dreams. My head aches, and I am burning from the inside out. The cold air of the cemetery makes my lungs hurt, so I pull my turtleneck up over my nose. That is warmer and gets sort of damp, but it does not hurt anymore. It is a dry cold, but the sky looks heavy with the threat of the first big snow. I cannot find a place to turn off the path, and I know Eliza will see me.

Then the hedges open up, like a secret passageway, and I veer in. Eliza will never find me here, *I am thinking, but then I trip over something and go sprawling. My landing sounds loud, so I curl up on my side and try to be quiet, listening. Eliza lopes by.*

I just want to be alone. I have all sorts of thoughts and feelings churning around inside of me so that I feel hot compared to the cold air outside. Eliza told me her dad got posted to Texas and they are leaving Germany. Her blue eyes do not even meet mine when she says it. I cannot speak, so instead I spin Flyer 180 degrees and run.

Now I uncurl and roll over on my back. I am surrounded by hedges, looking up into the lines of branches and beyond, to the gray clouds. I watch as they move, heavy and slow. I consider that they can obscure a dead person's view of her loved ones. I watch my breath disappear into the cold air. I count one two three four, and then I count by twos until my breathing slows.

I notice how comfortable my resting place is. It is padded with layers of leaves, and it is musty smelling, like the ground beneath Sebastian. I wriggle around to dig out a small space for my rump, and then I shake and nod my head, like yes no yes no, to make a hollow in the pillow of leaves for my head. It is totally quiet. I wonder if Eliza has gone on a current events field trip into the morgue without me.

Then I close my eyes, and I am in a huge field covered in snow, deep white cold snow, but it still smells like earth. I stretch out my arms to my sides and begin to make a snow angel, doing slow-motion jumping jacks, one two one two. I keep my eyes closed because I want the angel to be perfect, shaped perfect, a beautiful white-on-white angel from heaven laid down in this quiet hidden corner of the cemetery. Like my guardian angel.

Then my right foot bumps something. That will make my angel skirt lopsided, *I am thinking. I open my eyes and sit up.* What did I kick into? A rock? A big rock, I guess. *When I push away all the leaves from years of falls and winters and springs and summers, I can see writing. Something is engraved there: "Infant Girl. B 1958. D 1959. Our Sweet Angel."*

Then it hits me and I cannot breathe. I pull my turtleneck back up over my nose and try again. Still no breath. I throw back my head. I squeeze my eyes together, and then my hands cover up the headstone, and then a huge hard breath comes to me—stinging inside my chest— and I kick at the stone to push myself away. But I bump another one behind me. I am surrounded, and I almost jump up to run.

Then I see that there are other headstones, seven of them altogether. Now I can see them pushing up the layers of leaves. Now, when I pay attention, I can even see the texture of the headstones peeking through the darkness of the browns of the leaves and sticks and twigs and grasses, and a cold wind whips into my hiding place from the break in the hedges. Finds me there.

I scream, "Eliza! Come here. I'm back here. Hurry."
Silence.

"Eliza! Over here!" My throat is tight and my voice sounds like somebody else's. A big cloud of breath hangs in front of me, and I twist away from it. Finally I hear running steps on the gravel. "Over here!"

Eliza is there at the secret passageway, with blooming cheeks. I am still on the ground.

"What are you doing?" Eliza is breathing hard, and she looks huge from where I kneel.

"Look. You have to see this. Read this."

"What? So? Oh." Eliza stops. Then, "It's a baby." She drops to her knees beside the headstone.

"It's an American baby," I say.

Eliza is reading other stones. "These are all babies."

"I know," I say. "I was hiding in here, and I fell on a headstone. It's a mess in here. Why don't they rake it up?"

We both sit there for a moment, breathing hard.

Then Eliza says, "They're American babies. It's a German cemetery. Why should they?"

She stands up and disappears through the hedges, and I can hear her footsteps on the gravel, receding in the direction of home.

Doesn't she get it? These babies have been left behind. I sit there, and my mind goes blank. I cannot move either. Then I shake my head and deliberately make my eyes come into focus, and I realize that I am looking at the rockwork of an old wishing well.

I stand up and walk over to it, wondering what is at the bottom. I look in, and all I see is darkness. I place my hands on the rim so that I can lean over farther, and the rockwork crumbles beneath my fingers. There is no water. No ripples, no reflection, certainly no coins. It looks deep, but maybe that is an illusion.

"Hey!" I say, and then louder, "Hey, there!" to test the echo. But there is none. The wishing well is dead.

Then I get that creepy feeling, and I turn and run, to catch up with Eliza.

I match strides with her just as she is heading out of the pointy gates of the cemetery. The last thing I want to tell her about is the wishing well. I really want to forget about the whole place, the cemetery, the morgue, the baby graveyard—all of it.

Eliza is walking at quite a clip, and I have to hurry to keep up.

"Why are you in such a rush all of a sudden?" I ask. We're no longer on horseback.

"I need to talk to my dad."

"What about?"

"Just . . . I don't know," she says.

We keep walking, not galloping, and my brain begins to hurt with all the thinking I am doing while at the same time not accomplishing any great thoughts. How does all of this connect? What is going on in Eliza's mind?

Then I have a moment of clarity—finally.

"Wait. Eliza, remember you're spending the night?" I say. "Remember our dads have that meeting until late? And you're going to eat with us and stay over?"

She slows down. "Oh, right," she says, and at first I think I have disappointed her terribly. But then it is as if the sun has burst through the clouds and she grins. "Let's go to my house and get my stuff! I can talk to my dad tomorrow."

We make it to her house and collect her stuff and then go back to my house and up to my room, where we play with our horse statues until dinner. Everything seems calm and normal until we settle down on my bed later to read. Eliza is becoming jittery. Her hands are sort of shaking. Even though she is wearing a flannel nightgown, I figure maybe she is cold.

"It's freezing tonight," I say, trying to open an avenue for her to tell me what is up. "I bet it won't get this cold in Texas."

"No, it's a lot farther south."

"It will be hot down there."

"Hot as hell," she says, and we laugh, but then suddenly she stops. "I don't want to go to Texas," she says. "I don't want to leave."

I do not want her to leave either. We are best friends and there is no way to know if we would ever see each other again. Texas is so far from here.

Eliza slumps down on the bed, and her nightgown along with my feather blanket seem to swallow her up. I have never seen her this sad and dejected, so I try out an idea on both of us.

"When I move back to the States, I'll come visit you right away. I mean, that very summer," I say. Eliza does not respond at all. She lies there with a frown, her eyes focused on some vague distant spot way beyond my closet doors.

"No, that's not it," she says finally. "No." And then she straightens up and pulls her legs underneath her so that she can perch on them.

"What I mean is," she says, looking directly at me, "if I move, the spell will be broken."

The spell? I have not heard this before. I like the sound of it, until I consider that the whole thing is bad news.

"Things will change," she says. "Things will break. Things will be different."

Now Eliza is no longer looking at me; she is looking through me. I sit perfectly still. I feel tethered to her, somehow hung on the line of her vision, between what is real now and what she wishes for her future.

"Philippa, the worst can't happen here in Germany," she says. "See, I've thought it all through. I've thought of all the worst things that can happen, and since I can't predict the future, those things won't happen. I mean, it's never what I think it will be. You get it?"

"You mean about your mom? And if you stay in Germany, she won't die?"

Eliza focuses on me. Did I say the wrong thing? Was that mean? I hold my breath.

"Yes," she says. "Yes, that's it. Exactly."

"That's the spell?"

"That's the spell." She wraps her arms around herself.

I want to know more. I want to open this door farther, to look inside, like looking into the goomey lady's room, like opening the door to the morgue. It feels to me like the time has come for Eliza to open up; that is, if we are both brave enough.

"Have you told this to your dad?" I ask.

"No. But I know what he'll think about it."

"But wait. You just said you can't predict—"

"Not specifically, but I know how his mind works," Eliza says. "I know he'll want to protect me from my fears, so he'll try to distract me with something else. You know, like getting a horse when we get to Texas."

I think of my mom and her moonbeams—a gathering of silver from heaven—and I wonder if all parents try to protect their children from their fears. Not just the things they fear but the actual feeling of fear. I consider voicing that but decide it's not the right time. Moments pass.

"Philippa?" Eliza says.

"Hmm?"

"I have been wanting to thank you."

"For what?"

"For not making me talk. For just listening, like now."

"Oh, that," I say, stopping to consider. "But I thought maybe I was letting you down..."

"You remember how I told you I go to the cemetery to think? Well, I figured out that if my mom dies here, we'll have to bury her in the German cemetery. And leave her here when we move back to the States.

But since I thought of it, it won't happen. You see?"

Eliza is standing on the bed now, and her hands are gently chopping the air as she speaks. I want every word she says to be true.

"I've imagined it, the whole thing. It can't happen now," she says. "So if we stay here in Germany, Mom won't die."

But somehow the tone of her voice betrays her, and we both know it is not a guaranteed truth. Eliza does not have that power. Nobody does. She slumps back down into the feather blanket, and it looks like she has fallen into a ten-foot drift of cold white snow.

The Blue Feather, 1969

"YOU SLEPT LATE," said my mom. "You must have really needed the sleep. You're probably having a growth spurt."

I had come downstairs into the dining room to a table full of breakfast dishes, and I could hear the twins already playing outside. Their giggles and shouts did nothing to dispel my lousy mood.

I did not answer my mom and poured myself a bowl of cereal instead. Was I remembering right—about last night? Or was it just a dream? Did I ride Kirsch? Did Stefan kiss me? *Kuss?*

Then the phone rang, and it was Eliza.

"Whatcha doing?" She sounded in a really good mood. "Can I come over later, like after lunch?"

"Yeah, fine," I said.

"Let's go to Oktoberfest," she said, ignoring the glum tone of my voice. I knew she was trying to maintain her high, and I hated myself for being so uncooperative. I didn't know why she was so happy.

"No, I don't want to go there." I could not believe my words, but I kept on. "They're leaving, so why bother? Let's go to Sebastian's Woods."

"What? You don't want to see Kirsch? Why not?"

"I just don't. Come on. I'll see you when you get here."

We hung up, and I finished my cereal and tried to turn my mood in a hot bath. I put some bubble bath under the tap of streaming steaming water, and then I got in and let the bubbles completely cover my body. I closed my eyes and tried to imagine that I was back in the ocean, at the beach in Hawaii, and that I was only eight, and that all this weird confusing stuff had never happened. But it didn't work. I couldn't trick myself. I was living in Germany. I was almost 14. I was alienated from my best friend, even from myself. I sunk under the warm water and stayed there until I ran out of breath.

I grabbed a blue feather whip and was out the door the minute Eliza knocked. She hurried to keep up with me, her lime-green feather whip cutting through the chilly air. We walked side by side, with matching strides, and I concentrated down at our cords, the way our legs sprung out in front of us, the ground moving beneath. Our matching maxi coats were unbuttoned and the heavy purple fabric flowed behind us.

"What's with you?" Eliza asked.

"What's with *you?*" I countered.

We kept walking toward Sebastian's Woods. Minutes passed, filled with only the sound of our cords rubbing together and the rustling leaves that we kicked ahead of ourselves. When we got to Sebastian, we took up our positions, sitting side by side, leaning on him.

"I saw my mom last night," Eliza said. I did not say anything, because I could tell she wanted to talk. I think she wanted to break the tension between us. I was not sure how cooperative I would be. "She was better. She was calmer." Eliza pulled in some air. "She even kissed me."

"Stefan kissed me too," I blurted.

"What?"

"Did he ever kiss you?" I said, my voice speeding up, getting louder. "You know him from last year, don't you? Because I get the feeling that you. . ."

"Philippa, what happened?"

Then I began to cry.

"What's going on?" Eliza said. "Tell me!"

And then it all came tumbling out.

"I rode Kirsch. Stefan let me ride her in the ring. I wanted you to get to ride her too, but you weren't there. And then I brushed her and fed her, and it was the best, you know?"

I wiped my coat sleeve across my face and looked at Eliza, met her eyes for the first time that day. They looked bluer, more vivid than ever. I realized I had been avoiding looking at her. I was mad at her because I felt locked out of her world. She looked at me, and I could tell she was on the verge of crying too.

"He never kissed me," she said. "I never let him get that close."

"Why?" I asked.

"I don't know," she said, but she did know. "He's a German boy. He belongs here, and I don't. I didn't want to…. Especially with my mom being sick."

I didn't know what to say. She had thought it all through. I wanted to be able to think like that and to be so smart.

"Besides," she said, "I haven't had many friends, you know. I mean, nothing against you, but I didn't even want to meet you. My dad made me."

"Oh. Well," I said, hearing a hurt tone in my voice.

"No, Philippa, it's not you. I wanted to be alone, you know? But my dad didn't think that was right. He gets all worried about me. But, you know, I'm glad we met."

We sat there, fidgeting with our feather whips. Sebastian's Woods was silent. We both sniffed at the same time, and I almost wanted to look at her and laugh, like it was one of those funny things that we liked to laugh at, and then everything could go back to normal. But instead I stroked the blue feathers of my feather whip and tried to think my way out of the embarrassment I was in. Was it such a big deal about Stefan? Eliza did not care about Stefan. Eliza cared about her mother. She wanted to tell me about what had happened. And instead I had—

Then we heard men's voices behind us. We had always been alone in Sebastian's Woods, or so we thought. We heard leaves crackling and twigs breaking and men's voices, and they were getting closer.

I ducked down beside Sebastian and yanked Eliza down with me. The urge to hide was so strong. The footsteps kept coming. We huddled down closer to the ground with our heads touching, and then we managed to crawl under Sebastian, where we were hidden by his bulk and the branches and leaves that were scattered about. We lay curled up together, like twins in the womb, with Eliza's back to me. Our breathing was uneven as we waited. I had a hot panicked feeling in my chest.

We should have run, I thought. *We should have gotten out of here while we could. Now what?*

From where we lay, I could not see the men, and I hoped they could not see us. But they kept coming and finally stopped about ten feet behind us, pretty close but out of my field of vision because I was too cramped to turn my head.

The panorama in the shadow of Sebastian was dark, but beyond our hiding place the terrain was brighter, populated by leaves, stumps, rocks, and fallen branches. There were several voices, but they were low so I could not make out any words. Every now and then one voice would get loud and mad, but I didn't know what it said, and the other voice would quit.

The men were smoking and drinking from a bottle. I could hear it slosh. They were probably drunk, and that felt threatening. I began to sweat. A lit cigarette dropped into the dry leaves. Eliza stayed still, and I could smell the cigarette smoke mingling with the fragrance of flowery shampoo in her hair. I wondered how long we would be trapped here, unable to move or even to talk to each other to make a plan.

The man with the angry voice spoke again, and when no one answered him he must have hit someone because I heard a thump to the ground. Right then, directly in my field of vision, a blue feather from my feather whip fell down, as if in slow motion, onto the brown tumble of leaves. It must have fallen from my feather whip onto Sebastian, and now it had been blown down by an errant breeze. I knew Eliza saw it too, because she sucked in a burst of air.

Then there was another yell, and one of the men walked off. I could hear him go. I pulled my legs up, tightening them around Eliza, to signal her to keep still. I heard the fallen man stand up, sniff and cough. Several other voices spoke quickly and sharply, and then all the men trudged off. Eliza slowly released her breath, and when we were sure everyone was gone, we crawled out from under Sebastian.

We looked at each other and took turns wiping the leaves and sticks from our clothes and hair, except I left one stick poking out from behind Eliza's ear to give us something to laugh at. I realized I was not angry with her any more. For a few moments we did not speak.

"Sebastian to the rescue," I said, lamely, to fill in the dead space. I realized it wasn't our woods anymore.

"Let's get out of here," said Eliza. "This place is getting creepy."

But we both stood our ground. There was something unspoken hanging in the air, and I felt for once that I could grasp it and give it voice. I reached down and picked up the renegade blue feather.

"She kissed you?" I said, waiting for Eliza's eyes to meet mine.

She looked at me, and her blue eyes sparkled with tears again and she looked hopeful.

"Here," I said, handing her the blue feather. "For your box."

Then she broke into a huge grin and spun around, her heavy blond hair flowing out around her like the swings on the huge twirling swing ride.

"Come on," she yelled, and we feather whipped our horses into a gallop and ran from Sebastian's Woods.

The Spell Is Broken

SEBASTIAN'S WOODS IS the place Eliza and I go to get lost, to escape *anything based on reality. We are innocent and shouldn't have to struggle with things like loss and fear and pain. Yet. I squeeze my eyes to keep them shut. I have the feeling of consciously keeping myself unconscious. Scary thoughts could get the upper hand. I cannot allow myself to awaken. I want to remember.*

"I think that there are other girls like us all over the world, and there have been forever," I tell Eliza. She is sitting cross-legged in the fallen leaves and I am kneeling on Sebastian, fidgeting with a stick.

She looks up at me with an expression that seems to say, Where did that come from? *I look back at her like,* Heck if I know. *Then I go on.*

"Really, don't you think so? Think about it. Here we are, best friends in the middle of the Schwarzwald," I say. "We're just specks in here. We're just a pair among lots of other pairs, and in some ways they are just like us. I mean, those girls have to be just like us. And that's only now. I mean, think of all the years that have gone by. Lots of girls, lots of girls like us."

I am getting inspired, and Eliza is listening. Maybe she thinks I am a nut, but she's listening.

"Where are you going with this?" she asks. She is not annoyed or angry. She wants me to get to the point. If there is one.

"Nowhere, I guess. I was just thinking," I say. "Being out here with Sebastian takes me out of time, I think. I guess I'd rather let my thoughts drift sometimes than have them attached to hard things, concrete things."

"Like what concrete things?"

"Oh, I don't know," I say, trying to corral my ideas. "Like your move to Texas. Like you without your mom. Like me without you when you leave. Like us without Sebastian and Kirsch."

Then we are both silent, thinking.

"I mean, we really have to face it," I say, finally. "All this stuff is inevitable."

"Philippa, you can face it if you want."

It seems like she is going to continue with something like, But I'm not. The cool air around us is suddenly heavy with waiting.

"But?" I offer, to encourage Eliza to continue.

"But what?" she answers.

"Well, what are you going to do? I mean, how are you going to handle all this?" I say.

"Philippa, believe me. I'm already way beyond this. It's handled. It's done. I may be only 13, but I know what I can control and what I can't."

"So what about the spell?" I ask.

"Oh, please. That's old news," she says. "You don't really believe in spells, do you?"

What? Have I been asleep all this time? I hadn't realized that Eliza was reconciled to so much so quickly. How does she do that? What supernatural powers does she have that allow her to internalize everything and then accept it all? I feel as if I am always struggling with acceptance.

I guess I look stunned and downtrodden, because Eliza speaks up to console me.

"Philippa, look. I'm going to write to you every day." She pauses and reads my expression. "Okay, not every day but a lot. We can keep close contact until you move back to the States, and then you can come visit me, like you said."

Suddenly I am embarrassed for being so disarmed. I force myself to act cheered up.

"Okay. That's a plan. That'll work. We'll probably come back to the States in a year or at the most two. And then I'll come to San Antonio."

"Yeah," she says. "You'll come to San Antonio and I'll show you around. I'll show you the Alamo."

I don't know what that is, but I'll follow Eliza anywhere. And I follow her from Sebastian's Woods for the last time.

Negerkussen, 1969

I WOKE UP the next morning with a strange unbalanced feeling. Something felt off-kilter, but I could not put my finger on it at first. Then I remembered the incident with Eliza in Sebastian's Woods, the scary men and their drunken fight, and how our favorite place now felt so off limits.

I had no plans for the day, even though it was a Saturday. Eliza and I had not set anything up, and my mom was already busy at her desk so I knew I would have to watch the twins. They occupied themselves for most of the morning, building a hideout with blankets pitched over the furniture, and then I fixed tomato soup and floating crackers for lunch.

I could feel cabin fever coming on. I felt trapped indoors, and I needed to get out. I stuffed a handful of pfennigs into my pocket and told the boys we were going to the goomey store. They shot out the door without their coats, so I had to chase them down and dress them right, and then we marched off, each of my mittened hands clutching one of theirs.

"What are you guys going to get?" I asked. I was trying to focus on something real, something solid, imagining the bright yellow and red of the candies. I still felt spaced out, separated from the cold air by my buffer of coat, hat, and mittens. I tried to feel the warmth of the twins' hands through the protective fabric, but all I got was the gentle squeeze of their fingers.

"Yellow snakes!" said Quinn. He was continuing his experiment among the different goomey shapes but had not yet ventured from yellow. He had even asked for the color, *gelb,* but the goomey lady ignored that request. It worked out in the end, though, because August and I traded with him—and so did Eliza, when she came along. I guessed she was visiting her mom.

I squeezed August's hand so we could share a harmless joke about Quinn's color choice, and he smiled up at me.

"What about you?" I asked.

"I would like Negerkussen," August said, knowing that would steal my heart.

"Me too!" I said, and I lifted him up and spun him around.

"My turn!" yelled Quinn, so I spun him next.

"Come on," I said, and I grabbed their hands again so we could dash across the street safely together, across the tram tracks, and then down into the gulley.

We pushed open the door to the goomey store and were hit by a wall of overheated air. "Let's make it quick," I said, and my eyes immediately zeroed in on the tray of Negerkussen. "Just let me order, okay? I can get us in and out fast."

The goomey lady didn't come through the back door right away, which was unusual, so I decided I would show off for the twins and pretend to be her. I was going to walk around the glass case and stand behind it, scowling. I thought that would really crack up the twins. *But I had better hurry,* I thought, because I didn't want Frau Jaw to catch me. For some reason, the little sentinel dog was not there, so I figured I had some time.

Without a word to the boys, I hurried around to the back of the case, but something blocked my way and instead I sprawled onto the ground with an embarrassing *ka-thud!* I pulled myself up and peered over the top of the glass case, and I could see four eyes staring back at me. I got to my feet fast and realized that I had tripped on a step to a platform, and now I too towered over the candy case. So, Frau Jaw was not a giant after all.

"What are you doing, Philippa?" asked August, and I heard rustling in the back room, followed by the familiar yapping of the black rat dog.

"I don't know," I said and came back around to the front of the case. "I have no idea, guys. Okay, now hush!"

"Guten Tag," said the goomey lady as she came through the door,

well composed and seemingly oblivious to my antics. But something was different. Today she seemed calm, and her dog just stared at us, with no barking. Maybe he knew us by now. I met eyes with the goomey lady and I gave her a smile. She gave me nothing.

"*Guten Tag,*" I said, trying to sound nice. "*Drei* Negerkussen *und zwölf Schlange, bitte.*"

I kept it simple, ordering a Negerkusse for each of us and twelve goomey snakes. The goomey lady responded in slow motion, waiting a moment before stepping forward and taking her time to get a candy bag. And then I noticed the really different thing. She didn't have on the pink lipstick, and I saw then that she had such a tiny mouth. The boys watched closely as the goomey lady dug into the colorful tangle of snakes, grabbing a fair number of yellow ones, I noticed, for Quinn.

I paid and all three of us said, "*Danke.*" We were about to turn and leave when Frau Jaw spoke up.

"*Mädchen,*" she said, calling to me. And then she extended her hand, and in it she offered another Negerkusse. "*Für deine Freundin.*"

For your friend.

"*Danke,*" I said, feeling a smile cross my face. "For Eliza," I told the boys, opening my bag and allowing the goomey lady to add the Negerkusse to those already nested inside.

"*Danke,*" we all said again. "*Auf wiedersehen.*" And we left the hot room, letting the door thud shut behind us.

"Come on, guys," I said, suddenly feeling happy. "Let's sit at our special place and eat the Negerkussen."

It was almost too cold to sit in one place, and the overcast sky made the day seem even colder.

That was nice of Frau Jaw to think of Eliza, I thought, as I sat still, tasting the candy. *Maybe she's not so bad after all. Maybe I should not be so quick to make up nasty stories and jokes about her.*

We made fast work of the squishy Negerkussen, devouring them before the cold had a chance to stiffen the marshmallow, and one of the boys took the bag from me. I got caught up thinking about how maybe the goomey lady was just as nice as any other lady, and in that moment of distraction I let Quinn get away. August, as usual, had stayed near me, but Quinn's nature was to explore and he walked along the tram track embankment toward the place where it dropped off sharply. It took only a second and he was beyond my reach. And I hadn't even noticed.

I yelled for Quinn to stop right there. August and I scrambled to our feet, and I grabbed his hand. I thought Quinn would obey. He didn't.

"Quinn Swift! Come back here!" I yelled. "Listen to me!"

He looked over his shoulder as he ran. And then he was gone. I dropped August's hand and ran to the ledge, and my stomach lurched. There was Quinn, crumpled up in his coat at the bottom of the ditch.

His eyes were closed and he was terribly still. He looked so small. August yelled his name, and I held him back from going down too. I had to figure out how to get down there. It was steep and rocky. I could jump down the way Quinn had fallen, but it was hard to judge where I would land and I did not want to land on him. So I told August not to budge, and I worked my way down through a jumble of winter-bare saplings and fallen leaves, calling to Quinn, grabbing anything that would prevent me from falling down myself. August was sobbing pretty loud by then and intermittently screeching for me, but Quinn didn't awaken. When I reached him, I was afraid to move or lift him, so I fumbled with the collar of his jacket, put my cheek next to his, called to him softly. But nothing.

Then I realized I had no choice but to lift him out. I worked my arms under him, supporting his neck and back, and his eyelids fluttered. Somehow I was able to crawl with him, kind of drag him, up the wooded incline to where August stood, shivering and whimpering. Quinn was awake, but I carried him. August was pawing at me, so I got him on my back and I carried both boys home that way. I stopped to rest twice, and my arm muscles ached and my shoulder muscles burned. Even my legs, strong from running, were trembling. We were all three crying when I collapsed on the living room floor, laying the boys down at my mother's feet.

She immediately dialed emergency, and then she spun me around, held my shoulders, and asked what happened. I told her about the fall, and then she asked about August, who had finally stopped crying. It was then that I noticed he still clutched the candy bag after all we had been through.

"He's okay, aren't you, August?" I said and then heard the sirens. The ambulance people put Quinn on a stretcher and wheeled him into the truck. We followed in the car. Daddy was there when we arrived, but he didn't look at me. He was focused on Quinn.

I could not talk anyway. Everything was happening so fast. Each person had a job that they carried out with no wasted motion. My own existence in comparison was a pathetic slow-mo. I sat in a plastic chair in the hall, with August slumped on my lap, the bag of candy in his.

Finally, Daddy came to talk to me. I dreaded that he would tell me the worst, that because of my lapse, Quinn would die or something.

"Philippa, come on," said Daddy. "Come to my office."

I looked over my shoulder as I followed Daddy to the elevator, and I saw my mom come through a door into the hall and take August's hand. He stood there, so small, watching me go. I think he thought I was in trouble. I gave him a little wave so he wouldn't worry. I stepped into the elevator and the door slid closed.

"Where were you when this happened?" asked Daddy, looking straight ahead.

"We went to the goomey store. For candy."

"What's the goomey store?"

"It's where Eliza and I go to get candy."

"Off post? By yourselves?" he said, as the elevator door opened. He was tall, and he tended to lean toward me when he talked. But now he stood straight and looked at me hard.

He did not wait for me to answer but turned down the hall toward his office. I knew where to go because I had been to his office before. It was small, and he went around his desk to sit in his chair. Now we were eye to eye. I just stood there, feeling out of place, on the spot. I stared at his name plate: "Dr. Swift." Then I noticed a chair and sat on its edge.

"He's going to be alright," said Daddy, and that helped me relax. "We'll keep him here for the night just to watch him. He might have a concussion. We'll keep an eye on him. So he's alright, okay?"

"Okay," I managed.

Then he locked my eyes to his. "Philippa, I know you have a lot of responsibility with the twins. Your mom and I get that."

I looked down, twisting the hem of my sweater in my fingers, studying the yarn, saying nothing.

"But this..." he stopped. I looked up. "This could have turned out much worse. I can't have you leaving the post with the boys if you don't keep them with you all the time. This isn't a game, just playing with the boys. It's a big job that takes a lot of attention and maturity."

"I know," I said.

"They're getting bigger too, and it's a lot to keep up with."

Silence.

"Philippa?"

I thought about how this was the first time Quinn hadn't heeded my call. I didn't like that.

"Yes. I can do better," I answered. "I... I got distracted."

"You were daydreaming, I guess," he said, with a tone that suggested daydreaming was not unexpected but was forgiven. I realized that my negligence and the twins' increasing independence were a risky combination. "You have to be careful. You're growing up too, and life just gets more dangerous."

Just then, another doctor came in with some papers. He ignored her for the moment. "Don't go off the post anymore. Not unless you let me or your mother know," he said.

This didn't sound good to me. I felt reined in. As if in response to my thoughts, Daddy said, "This isn't meant as punishment, Phil."

Then he turned his attention to the woman. I didn't listen to their conversation. Instead, I heard a buzz in my ears. Somewhere inside of me I felt a switching of gears. My dad was asking more of me at the same time as restricting me. It felt confusing.

"Let's go upstairs and see Quinn," Daddy said. He was oblivious to my quandary because I didn't argue or defend myself anymore. And he took my hand as we walked to the elevator. He hadn't taken my hand since we moved to Germany. His hand was warm and big, and I liked holding it.

Quinn was sitting up in his hospital bed. He looked rosy and well. Mom was sitting in a chair with August in her lap. When he saw us, he pulled from Mom's grasp to join Quinn on the bed.

"Okay, easy, boys. Take it easy," Daddy said. My mom stood up and went to Daddy, and they spoke quietly to one another. My mom looked drained, and she leaned into my dad. She looked at me and gave a weak smile, so I knew she wasn't mad at me.

But I knew this was my fault. I swallowed hard and acted casual so that Quinn would not feel bad for me.

I hugged him and said close to his ear, "I'm sorry, Quinn. I'll have to take better care of you." I wasn't going to scold him.

"I fell down!" he said.

"I know," I said, for everyone to hear. I felt the need for everyone to know what we did, to know we had an adventure and that it wasn't all bad. "I fell down too, remember? I fell down in the goomey store!"

That reminder was all August needed to yank open the bag and thrust a yellow goomey snake into Quinn's face. I watched the boys play with their goomey snakes, and I felt relieved that they both seemed okay.

Then Daddy motioned me out of the room.

"Eliza wants to see you," he said, and I went into the hall. I saw Eliza peeking out from one of the far doorways, so I quickened my step and left my family behind.

Eliza looked fresh and bright-eyed. I imagined I was a mess after what had happened, but if she noticed, she didn't say. I wanted to see what was beyond her in the room. I knew her mother was there, and I wanted a glimpse. Eliza leaned casually against the doorjamb, blocking my view. "Is Quinn okay?" she asked.

"Oh, he's good. He's okay," I said. "How's your mom?"

"She's sleeping, and she's been really calm today," Eliza said. "I'm about to go home."

I stood there, hoping Eliza would allow me to see her mother, this woman who was dying, who was one day calm, one day agitated, and from what Eliza told me, not really all there. I had seen a woman alive. I had seen a woman dead. But I had never seen one halfway between.

"You can come in," Eliza said, and she pushed up straight from leaning on the doorjamb. It took a second for that permission to register in my brain, and then Eliza stepped aside and I passed through.

Eliza's mother's condition looked so different from Quinn's. He was young and vital—there was a sparkling energy field around him. But Mrs. Romin was lying flat on the bed, sleeping, her thin face pale and her chest rising regularly, short and shallow. I stood still, afraid to move nearer but also afraid to hurt Eliza's feelings if she saw my hesitation. I pushed away my memory of the morgue and those cadavers.

"You can get closer," she said, as if I were a shy pup that needed coaxing.

We walked right up to the bed. It wasn't so bad. I could smell lilacs, as if from a body powder. Mrs. Romin was sleeping under pastel blue sheets and a periwinkle cotton blanket, definitely not hospital issue. She was wearing a soft white cotton nightgown with a narrow ruffle around the collar. Her smooth eyelids were nearly translucent and laced with delicate blue veins.

"Isn't she beautiful?" Eliza asked.

At first I could not see it, her beauty, and I struggled briefly with how to respond. But then my perception adjusted and I clearly saw it. I saw what Eliza saw. I could hear her mother breathing. Her hair was brushed back from her face and fell in gentle waves on the pillow. The lines of her face were smoothed in relaxation.

"Yes," I said, believing. "She is beautiful."

Eliza leaned down and kissed her on the forehead. Then we turned to leave the room. Once out in the hall, we headed toward Quinn's room and August came bounding toward us, with my mom close behind. He had the candy bag, and he dug into it and brought out Eliza's Negerkusse.

"For you!" he said. What he held in his hand looked more like a half-baked mess of cupcake than the smooth sculptural Negerkusse it had been before the incident. But Eliza recognized it for what it was.

"*Mmmm,* thanks!" she said, and she managed to nab the blob of candy and devour it in one swoop.

"Oh, my gosh. Thank you," she said again after she swallowed it. "I needed that."

August stared at her with a smile. And then I saw something pass behind his eyes, a great idea, and he reached into his coat pocket. Out came his hand, clutching a red goomey snake. He held it out to Eliza.

"Here, Eliza," he said. "Give this to your mommy."

"Thank you, August," she said. "She will love it."

PART II

Spin the Bottle, 1970

ELIZA AND HER family moved to San Antonio. I wrote to her once, but she never wrote back. Finally, right around when school started, my family and I got a card from her dad with a picture of Eliza standing in front of the Alamo, and she had written, "Wish you were here, Philippa!!" and signed her name with Xs and Os. There was a famous battle at the Alamo, according to an inscription on the back of the card, and a lot of people died. The catchphrase was "Remember the Alamo," so that you would remember who died and what they died for. I mainly hoped that Eliza would remember me.

I never knew how to keep up a friendship from a distance, and now it was happening with Eliza. When I sat down to write her a letter after that first one, I went blank. What could I say? What was interesting in my life? I didn't have a horse. I didn't have any friends. I didn't do anything that was fun.

I had no control over Eliza's leaving, and now I felt helpless to communicate with her. I never talked to anyone about it, and I must have kept a good poker face, because my mom never brought it up.

Meanwhile, August and Quinn were growing up and away from me, becoming slippery in my arms and shrugging off my kisses. I missed their fawning gazes. They had started school, and so a whole new world opened to them. They began testing my authority. Quinn's escapade was only the beginning. So rather than fighting with them, I gave up, gave them back over to my parents.

There was one thing that gave me hope. My dad had been notified that we were being stationed in Texas too, and we would leave for the States after school was over. I knew it would be a big change in my life. I mean, besides the move back to the States. I would get to see Eliza, number one, and I was finally going to get a horse of my own. That was a promise I never doubted.

But meanwhile I had to get a life here in Germany to make it through the school year. I had devoted myself so strongly to my friendship with Eliza that I excluded all other possibilities, and now all the other girls had best friends already. I felt adrift, but I did not feel prepared to take on a best friend anyway. I did not think I could connect with anyone again as strongly as I had with Eliza. In some ways, it was easier to be a loner.

Every now and then I hung out with a couple of fringe girls—that is what I called them—who were independent enough not to need much from me. I mean, not that I told them I called them fringe girls. It would probably insult them. They did not hang out in cliques, and that meant they were not "popular." Usually I noticed them outside of groups, alone, reading maybe. When we got acquainted, sometimes I went to their houses for lunch during school or saw them on weekends at the movies or the PX, but mostly I kept to myself and my horse statues.

But the joy in my imaginary horse world was disintegrating. The statues had lost all their animated qualities. They used to be alive to me, with personalities and funny habits. Now they were solid and lifeless. I had to work hard to remember what Kirsch looked like, and I figured out that I had only a month to wait before the Oktoberfest came back to town. I would get to see Kirsch, with her black eyes and white eyelashes, and Stefan. Stefan with his green eyes. But for now life was a bore. I had become a fringe girl myself.

Then one fringe girl, Chris, who had a freckled nose and wore her hair cropped short, invited me to an AYA dance on a Saturday night. The AYA was the American Youth Association, just for us army brats. I didn't know if it was a fancy thing, so I asked Chris what she wore. She said, "Just jeans or whatever."

Early one Saturday night I got on the smelly fatigue-green bus that drove us out to the AYA. The air was brisk outside, but inside the bus was stagnant and humid. Nobody looked up at me as I made my way down the aisle to a seat in the back. It reminded me of the German tram. I almost chickened out entirely and bagged the idea, but as the diesel engine labored into full throttle I let the motion toss me into a seat. I slid toward the window and stared out, totally ignoring the conversations of other kids. I let my hair hang down on either side of my face, like blinders. I was beginning to get the hang of being fringe.

The AYA dancehall was cavernous, but black lights ignited psychedelic posters on the walls. My cords were dark, but my shirt had some colors that popped in the lights. Images of Jimi Hendrix, peace signs, and sayings like "Make Love, Not War" decorated the posters and set a rebellious mood that somehow made me feel more comfortable in the role of being aloof and defensive.

A band was setting up and kids milled around aimlessly and embarrassed, drinking Cokes from sweating bottles. Some of the older kids even smoked cigarettes, and a haze was building. No one made eye contact. I found a random chair against a wall and sat down. No reason to be self-conscious because no one was looking at me, as if I were invisible. I saw some of the kids from school, but they were too involved in their cliques to notice me. The girls kept looking down at their bodies to be sure they looked right, and the boys were in a constant struggle with their long hair, wanting it to hang loose around their faces but being annoyed by it at the same time. Then Chris spotted me and came over. She leaned against the wall beside me and slid down until she was sitting on the floor, and she stretched out her legs and crossed them at the ankle.

"How's it going?" she asked. She was so relaxed and casual. I tried to calm myself and mimic her. I thought she had this loner thing down pretty well. She was wearing jeans that were faded from wear and a long necklace of dark-colored glass beads.

"Okay," I said. The band was beginning to tune up, and the drummer was adjusting the heights of his instruments and tapping and pounding in turns. The band was made up of high-schoolers, with a tall black singer who closed his eyes and held the mike with both hands, saying, "Testing, testing," adjusting it. He couldn't get it up to his height, so he cocked one hip and sort of leaned into the mike from the side while he tested it. I found myself staring at him. I did not know why, but I guess I had never seen a guy with his moves and air of confidence so close up there on stage. Plus his being on stage gave me permission to stare. Chris noticed.

"That's Michael," she said.

"What?" I said, and then, embarrassed, I ad-libbed, "Oh, yeah. I can't imagine being on stage, can you?"

"What do you mean?" she said. "I've seen you on stage before."

Busted. Chris caught me in a lie. I did not know what to say, and I sat there for a moment, hoping that somehow the conversation would get interrupted or derailed. I fixated on the dusky glow of Michael's skin.

"You know, the talent show," she continued. "You and that blond girl. You played 'Born Free' on the guitar and you both sang."

I could hardly stand the embarrassment. It was bad enough that day on stage. I was so scared that I could barely fill my lungs with air to sing and my guitar playing was wooden and awkward. Eliza and I both felt like we must have blacked out or something—we could not remember anything about the performance afterward, and later we kept giggling, not really talking about it, until we could let the subject totally drop and pretend it never happened. But obviously Chris remembered.

"Oh, right," I said. "That."

"What. You were good," she said. "They could have turned up the mike a little."

"Do you sing?" I asked, to distract her.

"Yeah, I sing sometimes," she said, turning her head toward the stage. "With Michael."

"You do?" I said, and I realized my voice sounded so childish and eager, completely out of synch with the teenage surroundings. "That's cool," I said, in a more casual tone.

Chris nodded and then got to her feet. "Come on," she said. "Let's get a Coke."

Once the band started up, I did not have to worry about sounding stupid anymore, because you could hardly understand anyone at all. With the exception of Michael, who had this cool stage presence, the band was real loud and rowdy, long hair flying every which way, sweaty faces, lots of stage antics. But Michael took it nice and easy. We all stood around listening to the music, and I continued to stare at him. I stayed back against the wall so no one would notice me. Through it all, he was relaxed and composed, leaning forward slightly to deliver his lyrics into the mike.

When he sang "The Boxer," by Simon and Garfunkel, his delivery was hypnotic: "By the light, by the li li li li light, by the light..."

Chris went on stage and sang a song with him, the last song in the set. She had to stand tiptoe to reach the mike, but it gave her a look of urgency that I liked, as if she was really making an effort and sounding good in the process, such a contrast to my stage performance. She had all the moves, and I realized I admired her. When the band took a break, Michael came over to where I was sitting with some other kids, in a circle on the floor. I sat there because I couldn't find a chair. The kids all knew each other, so I thought I would blend in by acting like I did not care that no one was talking to me. The speakers played some of the hits on the Stateside Sound Survey, but not as loud as the band played. I acted nonchalant.

At one point I left the group to grab another Coke, and when I got back someone was spinning a Coke bottle in the middle of the circle. *So this is Spin the Bottle,* I thought, and sat back down in the circle where I had been. It would have been too obvious to turn away, would have made me seem so chicken. I sat Indian-style, catty corner from Michael. In that position, I could lean back enough behind the person I was sitting next to so as to block his view of me. I was getting self-conscious again.

I thought, *What am I doing?* I wondered, *Why am I in this circle?* I realized, *I want to be kissed.*

Michael spun the bottle, and it started as a blur and then stopped, its mouth pointing at me. There was no doubt. Everyone looked at me. I surprised myself by not hesitating. I leaned forward and met Michael's eyes. *This is it,* I thought. I rose toward Michael on my knees, and our lips met in the black light. His lips were soft and big, and they were closed. He didn't touch me with his hands. It took only an instant.

"Where it's at," he said, quietly enough so that only I could hear, and smiled.

Then we moved back to where we had been, but Michael was still smiling at me. He had doe eyes and a shy smile, shy for a guy who could really sing on stage.

For the rest of the night the touch of his lips on mine was all I could feel, or see or hear, for that matter. I was not in love with Michael, but I knew I had discovered something new, something that had been right in front of me all along, ready for me whenever I was ready for it. I kept away from the circle for the rest of the evening, because I could not stand for anything to ruin it. I wanted to keep my lips untouched and pouting, to make the kiss last forever. I figured no one would miss me.

Later, I rode the bus back to the post, looking out the window at nothing, at the darkness, and instead churning the memory of the kiss through my mind. I did not love Michael, but I loved his kiss. That kiss had been nice and warm. That kiss had been sweet and welcome. Not at all like the angst-filled kiss with Stefan, light-years ago. Back when I was not ready. Every now and then lights from outside the bus illuminated my face so that I caught glimpses of my reflection in the window, like a slow-mo flickering movie. Was I changing? I did not recognize myself in that stuttering light.

When I got home, I went into my parents' bedroom to tell my mom that I was back. Daddy was at the hospital, so Mom was in bed alone. The lights were out, and she was breathing softly.

"Mom, I'm home," I whispered.

"Okay. How was it?" she whispered back, turning onto her side so she could face me. I could see her eyes in the dark. I could tell she was interested.

"Good. It was fun. Mom, my hair smells like smoke, but I didn't smoke."

"Okay. Go to bed now. Shampoo it in the morning."

The Fever

"PHILIPPA." I FEEL gentle smacks on my cheeks. "Wake up, Flip. Can you hear me?"

I feel so far away. I feel exhausted, like I am at the bottom of a deep well and it is impossible to ever come back to the surface. I refuse to make the effort to come back to my body. My body is still on James's couch, and the hammer is still on my head.

"Philippa."

"Let's take her to the hospital."

"Where? You mean emergency?"

"She's burning up."

I feel a cool wet cloth on my forehead. Cool water drips down my temples, and behind my ears it becomes warm. I feel nauseous again.

"I want to go home," I say.

"I know where she lives."

The voices recede. I take a deep breath and sigh. Hands are beneath me, lifting me.

A New Friend, 1970

MY PARENTS FOUND a "new friend" for me who had horses. Maybe they actually had noticed my low mood after Eliza left, or maybe it was just luck. Anyway, the father was scheduled to pick me up at the end of his workday on a cool fall Friday. He was American and his wife was German. She was a patient of Daddy's. One day she mentioned her daughter and her horses, and that did it. So now the family had invited me to stay with them for the weekend so I could ride. Their daughter, Gabby, was a little older than I, but even though her English wasn't fluent, the idea was that we would communicate in the international language of adolescent horse-loving girls.

I was dubious and optimistic at the same time. What did I have to lose? At least I could get away from my boring life at home and be around horses again. Since Eliza left, my life had ground to a halt. Together we were always up to something, running off somewhere, cracking each other up. Now time dragged. The days of trading goomeys were over, and I couldn't ride Sebastian without Eliza jumping up and down on him. Maybe Gabby and her horses could make the difference for me.

Mr. Shore arrived right on schedule, and my mom shuttled me into the car. It was small and cramped, not the least bit luxurious. I had the feeling of excitement and dread, and as usual my stomach felt bad. The inside of the car smelled like cigarette smoke and gasoline, which made things worse for me. But I planted myself on the chilly seat and tried to look happy.

I waved bye to Mom and turned to give a smile to Mr. Shore so that he would get the car on the road. The Shores lived outside of Munich, and the trip would be about 45 minutes. Mr. Shore was tall and thin, with a bulbous forehead. He looked kind in a grandfatherly way, but to my dismay, he immediately lit a cigarette.

"I'll crack my window so the smoke won't bother you," he said, his Adam's apple bobbing. *Considerate but futile,* I thought. He drove through the city, and then we got on the autobahn, where we picked up speed. All the cars were going fast and weaving to get ahead of one another.

"Gabby is looking forward to riding with you," Mr. Shore said between drags on his cigarette. "Your father told Mrs. Shore that you're quite a rider."

"I love horses, but I haven't gotten to ride much since we came to Germany," I said.

"We'll fix that," he answered, and then I was relieved that for the rest of the trip he concentrated on his driving and smoking. I didn't want to have a conversation with him, because it felt so forced, and I didn't want to make any effort while feeling so bad. At least he wasn't driving like all those other crazy people. I gradually slinked lower in my seat so that I didn't have to breathe in the haze of smoke that was floating along the ceiling of the car. It looked like Mr. Shore's bald head was shrouded in clouds, the way a really big mountain looks when snow clouds are sinking low.

We finally got off the autobahn and slowed, negotiating neighborhood streets, and then Mr. Shore pulled the car into an enclosed garage. I struggled to open my door, and suddenly it was opened from the outside by a smiling girl with shiny red cheeks. She had this mischievous look that played about her eyes. I got the feeling that she had been waiting impatiently for me.

"Hello, nice to meet you, I'm Gabby," she said in a rapid-fire German accent. She held out her hand to shake. I stood up and grabbed her hand, and immediately my stomachache disappeared. Although the garage air wasn't fresh, it sure beat the suffocating atmosphere of that little car.

Gabby took my overnight bag and led me into the house, which had an odd smell of its own. I couldn't quite identify it—some foreign cleanser smell or some strange food. Then my queasiness began to come back when I caught a whiff of the dinner. It was wurst, I just knew it, and I hated wurst. Why do you think they call it wurst? It was the most disgusting thing to eat, with gnarly bits and chewy chunks and overwhelming spices in some cases, and I immediately regretted coming to stay with a family that was even part German. Why hadn't I foreseen that I'd have to eat German food like wurst?

"Ah, here you are," said Mrs. Shore, walking into the dining area in thick woolen socks. She looked considerably older than my mom and I thought how odd it was that she had a daughter Gabby's age. She carried all her weight in her bust and shoulders, which made her look heavy, but her body tapered down to skinny little legs and small feet. She was smiling broadly and she swept me up in her arms, like I was a child of her own. She was much more padded with flesh than my mom. "We are so happy to have you! Gabby can't wait to show you the horses." She pronounced her *w* like a *v*: "Ve are so happy" and "Gabby can't vait."

She released me from her embrace, and held me at arm's length. She was one of those ladies who draws on her eyebrows and always looks surprised. I stammered how happy I was to be here too and to get to ride. "Thank you so much for inviting me," I said. I wanted to be sure to say that.

"You make yourself at home. Gabriella vill show you ze room, and I vill put dinner on ze table!" she said. Her *th* sounded like a *z*. "I've made somezing special for you!"

Gabby and I looked at each other, and then I followed her down the hall to her room, thinking how off-base Mrs. Shore was if she thought I would consider wurst somezing special. I tried to shake off my ungrateful feeling along with my nausea. Gabby's room was dominated by a huge bed with a headboard that had shelves and cabinets.

"You sleep here," Gabby said, patting one side of the bed, "and I sleep there."

"Okay," I said.

Then she said, *"Komm,"* and I walked behind her to the dining room, where Mr. and Mrs. Shore were already seated.

"Ve are having vurst from Munich," Mrs. Shore said, with a tone that indicated to me that she thought I would be greatly impressed. "I'm sure you love it. And *Kartoffeln!*"

I did like potatoes, for sure, and they would save the day for me. I was able to smile eagerly as she forked over a big ol' wurst—white with black speckles made up of who-knows-what—and spooned the buttery hunks of potato onto my plate. I managed to cut a few small pieces of the wurst and hide it from myself in the potato that I piled onto my fork. Then, when I actually ate it, I avoided touching the wurst with my tongue so I didn't have to feel the gross texture, just letting my teeth do their work before I swallowed the whole mouthful. I did that about four times, and then I skipped the wurst part altogether, leaving most of my portion uneaten. When we cleared the table, I met eyes with Mrs. Shore, and she only said, "You must be excited to ride!"

I was. I couldn't express it, though. The thing was, I didn't know what it was like to own a horse, to go to the stable to see your own horse. In a way, I didn't know what to expect; all I felt was suspense, and it was exhausting.

"Mutti, may we make cupcakes now?" Gabby asked. She was so eager, and I guessed it had been their plan, something to do with me in the evening before bed. I was game. I loved to bake muffins and cupcakes. Eliza and I had made cupcakes every chance we got, like for birthdays and other celebrations.

Mutti finished the dishes and helped gather ingredients to add to the boxed yellow cake mix. Gabby and I took turns with the hand-held electric mixer, and we dipped our fingers into the batter for tastes, dodging the mixer blades and giggling. Mutti caught us and told us it was unsanitary, and she handed me a big metal spoon to clear the sides of the bowl. I had done that before, like with a stirring spatula, but Gabby and I didn't have the coordination together that Eliza and I had. I began to scrape down the bowl, and in a second the spoon was gobbled up by the whirring mixer blades. Gabby got startled and yanked up the mixer, and cake batter went everywhere. I froze in embarrassment and shame.

"I... I'm sorry," I said, looking at the twisted metal of the spoon and the mixer. I thought the thing must be broken beyond repair. Gabby just stared at the mess she was holding in her hands. Then she looked at Mutti, gauging her response.

"Macht nichts!" said Mutti, meaning it doesn't matter. Her drawn-on eyebrows jumped up in high arches, and she yanked out the two mixer blades to throw them along with the mangled spoon in the trash.

"Mutti!" said Gabby. She was astounded. "How do we finish the cupcakes?" Then she looked hard at me.

"Löffel!" said Mutti, and she handed us each a large spoon. Gabby seemed really put out.

"Was ist los?" Mutti asked.

Gabby turned her hard look on her mother. *"Macht nichts?"* she said. "Usually it really matters!"

Mrs. Shore ignored her. "It's okay, Philippa," she said, conspiratorially. "Don't vorry about ze mixer."

"I'm sorry," I said again, and I worried. Gabby was stirring vigorously, and I didn't bother trying to put in my spoon.

The cupcakes turned out pretty good, even without frosting, and Gabby did most of the pink and green sprinkles. I held back, still shaken with guilt and disoriented by the exchange between Gabby and her mother. I didn't take a second cupcake when Gabby pushed it my way.

"Philippa, what?" she said.

"I just feel bad about... the mixer."

Gabby laughed, finally. *"Pffft!"* she said. "Who cares? We'll get a new one!"

THE NEXT MORNING I woke up with none of my usual grogginess, and I had slept off those weird feelings from the night before. We had brotchen for breakfast, my favorite. I loved the crusty outside of the rolls, and I ripped them in half and piled on the sweet butter and purple jam. Mrs. Shore served tea with cream and sugar, with her usual high spirits. I got seconds of everything.

"Let's pack up for ze stables," said Mrs. Shore, and Gabby and I scrambled back to the bedroom. I pulled on my cords to ride, but Gabby frowned, as if they weren't the right thing to wear. I had forgotten that she had riding clothes for me to borrow. She handed me a pair of her breeches, and I pulled them on. They were really soft and stretchy, and they looked new. Then she pulled out some shiny high black boots from her closet, like Jurgen's big black boots, and a pair for herself too, only in brown. I could tell the Shores had a lot of money to spend on their riding.

The trip to the stables was short, and when we got there I felt blind to everything else until I was able to get a glimpse of Gabby's horses, especially the one I would ride. I had a one-track mind.

There she was, Forella, a chestnut mare, looking out of her stall with her ears straight up and her eyes bright. She had a white blaze with undulating edges that went from her forehead to the tip of her muzzle. Her socks were so white they shined silver. This was the closest thing to a horse of my own, even closer to being mine than Kirsch, it seemed. I felt certain that this was the most important moment of my life. I walked up close to her so that I could feel her warm breath. She nuzzled me gently, and we made friends right away. I didn't need any prodding or direction when it came to brushing her or tacking her up. Gabby and I went about our business, getting the horses ready, and then we walked them through the barn to the big indoor arena, with its vast heavy-sanded surface. It reminded me of the pony concession arena, only it was ten times as big and oval instead of round.

Gabby used a mounting block to get up, so I followed her. Forella and Gabby's gelding, Brav, were big horses, and I couldn't reach the stirrup much less grab the mane or saddle to pull myself up. Forella stood nicely in front of the block while I mounted her. I got my stirrups adjusted just right, and then we began to ride the horses in the big oval arena. I could hear Forella's tail swishing behind me, and gradually she warmed up and was eager to trot.

THE NEXT WEEKEND, I went to the Shore's again. Things were settling down and I was feeling more relaxed. But as I was climbing into the smelly little car for Mr. Shore to take me home, Mrs. Shore tapped me on the shoulder. I turned to her quickly once I sat down in the chilly seat, and she leaned toward the window. I rolled it down.

"Don't forget," she said, her eyebrows arching dramatically. "Next veek is ze show! You vill ride in ze equitation class on Forella."

"I..." I was at a loss for words.

What does she mean, don't forget? I didn't even know that I was riding in a show, so how could I forget something I never was even aware of?

"Don't vorry. It vill be fun!" Mrs. Shore and Gabby stood staring at me as the car putted backward out of the garage. Mr. Shore accelerated through the narrow cobblestone streets of the neighborhood, and the trip was a blur. At one point he might have said something, but I couldn't decipher it with the droning of the engine and my preoccupation with this problem of a show. I let an uncomfortable time pass before I answered—a muted "Excuse me?"—for not having understood. Mr.

Shore didn't respond. Then I abandoned answering at all. It was in the past, and I couldn't recover it. Mr. Shore didn't seem to mind, concentrating on the road and lighting cigarettes off one another as he reached each burning nub.

Then I spent all week twisting in agony about the prospect of the horse show. Nothing seemed to make me feel better. My mom said that she would come with the twins to watch and that I didn't have to think of it as a competition, just as a chance to show what I could do. But her words didn't make me feel better. I was terrified. All eyes would be on me. My nervousness would transfer through my thighs, and Forella would feel it and become jittery too. I would be judged for the detail of my riding. The judge would pick me apart, my head, my shoulders, my back, my hands, my seat, my legs, my feet. How could I possibly ride the way I usually do—with such freedom and happiness, such a sense of belonging—if I were being graded on my every move? I began to scheme up ways to avoid even going to the Shores' for the weekend. Maybe I'd be sick. Maybe I'd have a sore leg, I don't know, a sore back or maybe I'd claim the standard, a stomachache. But suddenly it became Friday evening, and now I was whisked away by Mr. Shore in his little car.

"Are you ready for the horse show tomorrow?" he said. "Gabby has kept Forella clean and groomed all week. You girls are in the same equitation class, you know."

"Oh, no, I didn't know," I answered lamely, hoping he'd stop talking about it.

"It's a big class," he said. I was silent, concentrating on the ribbon of road in front of me, how it unwinded ahead and then disappeared beneath. Mr. Shore took a deep drag on his cigarette and then, not bothering to blow the smoke, spoke, creating a disorganized exhalation of the gray noxious stuff. "You don't sound very excited about it. Are you nervous?"

"No. I, it's just..."

"Gabby was nervous for her first show too," he said, ignoring my denial. I didn't speak, waiting for him to light a cigarette off the burned-down one. It helped to occupy my mind, watching him with this trick. I was enthralled by how he kept the jetting car on the road, going so fast, while fidgeting with both hands at the top of the steering wheel to pry a cigarette from the pack and then get it lit. The car careened a bit between the lines on the road but from my perspective never went over into the wrong lane. I considered offering to help somehow, but then I didn't. I sat there, sort of helpless. I felt the weight of being a child, being able to see things for what they were but unable to fix or change them. After all, I didn't drive. I didn't smoke. And I sure didn't want to ride in a show.

Young Moons

IN MY OWN bed now, under my warm fluffy feather blanket, I feel safe but still hot and sick. I roll onto my side to face Eliza, who is beside me in my dream. We are hanging out in Sebastian's Woods. I remember piling leaves into a heap for cushioning and covering it with a green army blanket.

Eliza and I loll about, the leaves crunching beneath us, discussing important things and making things up. We are always making things up. It is how we explore what's in our hearts. Flyer and Posey, meanwhile, are calm, browsing along the forest floor, their muzzles twitching among leaves and twigs and finding occasional tender tufts of greenery.

"That was an adventure," says Eliza, pretending an exhausted exhalation. "Nothing like making a great escape under a full moon." She lies on her back, her head cradled in her arms and her eyes gazing upward.

I follow Eliza's lead, with the fiction: "The timing was risky. Planning is everything."

"But I'm glad we did it," she says. She waits a sec and then informs me, "I chart the moon."

"Hmm," I respond, letting her develop the story.

"So then I know when the night is darkest."

"On the new moon," I reply, because I know.

"On the new moon."

Eliza and I are moonies. We joke that we live in Moonich. We played around with a lamp, a globe, and an apple one day to figure out

106

how phases of the moon work. The key is to understand that from earth we see only one side of the moon. Ever. Because it rotates on its axis at the same rate it revolves around the earth.

"The moon has a dark side," I remind Eliza.

"Don't we all," she says.

"Eliza..."

"What. We do," she says, in a sweet tone, to console me. "Don't be so sensitive."

"Well, we know when the night is brightest," I say. Eliza is right about my sensitivity. I want to shake it off and appear casual. I toss in a curve: "Unless we're under a blanket of clouds, of course."

"A green wooly blanket of clouds..."

"Hah! A warm wooly blanket of clouds." Our easy rhythm has returned, and we both breathe easy and enjoy the calm silence of Sebastian's Woods. Hot in my bed, I kick the feather blanket clear of my legs.

"We were quite clever to put decoy pillows under our bedcovers, to look like us sleeping," Eliza says, rejoining our entertaining fiction.

Interesting idea, *I think. This is not even close to true, but it's so fun to act like it is. And I go along:* "Our parents will never know better."

And then we both think on that awhile. I mean, it is doable. A sneak-away campout under the stars in Sebastian's Woods.

"Seriously" Eliza says finally. "Let's do it sometime."

"On the new moon," is my answer.

"On the new moon."

James, 1970

"GET UP, PHILIPPA!" I heard my mom calling. "You need to get up."

There was that urgency in her voice again, that strained pitch, like she was angry or annoyed. I hated that being my first communication in the morning. I clamped the pillow over my head and tried to go back to sleep. Start over again fresh, waking up in my own time, clean, pure, golden.

But golden days were over. Everything had gotten out of synch. I could not do anything right anymore, and so whenever I talked to my mom we exchanged short angry words.

It all began when I came home from the AYA later than she expected. Later than my curfew, which was 10 o'clock, about when things got started, let's face it. I had finally made some friends, and I wanted more time with them. It was so boring to explain that my parents wanted me home early. On this night, as usual, Mom was in bed alone. I turned the face of her illuminated clock toward the wall.

"Mom, I'm home," I whispered.

She was slow to awaken, but when she did, she gave no indication she knew it was 10:23. Twenty-three minutes late does not seem like a lot. It does not seem like it should matter. But just to clinch it, I hid the time, so she would drift back off to sleep, like usual.

Which she did. And so I turned the clock back around and left the room. And then instead of going to my room, to bed, like I was supposed to, I went into the twins' room just to listen to their breathing. And then I crept down the stairs and left the house.

"We're good," I said to Angel, who was standing in the shadows of the carport. For a moment he looked like a statue, because the darkness had taken away all color and he was cast in grayish mottled stone.

"She sleeping?" he asked.

I nodded, and we grabbed hands and started running away from the house, toward the woods where the Oktoberfest was. We ran in step somehow. I was not cantering anymore, like I used to with Eliza. I was running like a human girl, not a horse, and we held hands until we began to tire, and then we released our grip and used our arms for balance and power and kept going, racing. And then when we got really tired, we slowed to a walk and joined hands again, and I said, "Here it is," as I led him to the playground that stood in a clearing, lit dimly by the contented grin of a crescent moon.

Angel was from California. That is if you could say that any army brat actually was from anywhere. Los Angeles. Hence the name Angel. He was born there but had moved all over, like I had. And now our paths had crossed, and I connected with him in a way that felt so natural and pure.

"So what's your real name?" I asked him, as we backed onto the swings, grasping the cold chains that tethered them to the set frame.

"Angel," he said, and we both hopped off the ground, leaned back with our legs outstretched, and flew forward on the swings.

"No," I laughed. "I mean, your birth name, the one you were given at birth."

"Okay, then. That's different," he said. "Because my real name here is Angel. But in LA, it was James."

"James." We continued swinging, and our tempos matched.

"Yep."

"So why don't you use James anymore?"

"Last year there were two other Jameses, so we all branched off. Those guys moved. Dallas and Jersey. But my name stuck."

"Angel. It works for you," I said, still swinging. "Look at you fly."

"Call me what you want." He pushed even higher.

"Come on," I said, feeling the tug of home. "I need to go back."

I did as dramatic a jump from the swing as I could, and Angel followed suit. He had a rough landing and almost bit the dust, but he recovered his footing and we ran off laughing.

When I turned my key in the front door, I immediately felt something was amiss. There stood both my parents in the front hall, my mom in her robe and my dad in his uniform. What was he doing home, anyway?

"Philippa, where have you been?" my mom asked.

"I just went out for a few minutes…" There was really no acceptable explanation.

"You were home from the AYA," she said. "I expected you to go to bed. Daddy checked on you, and you weren't there. What's going on? Who were you with?"

"It's eleven-thirty," said my dad. "You've been out for an hour."

I did not know what to say. My parents kept staring at me, but then I began to realize that neither of them had the energy to yell or to even get that mad, at least not right now. No likely lie occurred to me either. I could not come up with any better scenario than the truth.

"I just wanted to hang out with this guy."

Their faces changed. They looked suspicious. My dad scowled and my mom squinted her eyes.

"He's my friend. Don't make such a big deal about it, okay? It's alright."

"No, it's not alright, Philippa. We cannot have you sneaking out at night," my dad said. "It's not safe, and it's not right for you to be running around in the night with some boy."

"Okay, I won't do it again." I spun toward the stairs and ran up them. "I'm going to bed. G'night."

They did not say anything else or follow me upstairs. I thought I had gotten off scot-free. Until the next morning, when my mom woke me up and told me that she and my dad had decided to restrict me permanently from the AYA.

Good & Plenty

I REMEMBER WHEN I needed to get some cigarettes because I had only a couple in my pack. I can feel the pack, crushed in my front pocket because I still have on my tight cords, even though I am in my bed. My boy James brought me home. I turn onto my side and play it all out, like a movie in my mind.

I hurry down the stairs to the basement of the hospital, hoping there is no one around so I can grab some from the vending machine. I need extras—I do not even smoke them—so that when Angel asks for one, I will have it. Some girl gave me a pack to hold once at the AYA while she danced. When Angel asked, I yanked it from my pocket fast. It was like some weird reflex, like I did not even think about it and it happened. Life was a lot like that lately, things happening without my control. Fast, in a way that I cannot keep up with.

I watched Angel's face when I handed over the pack. His brows went up and then he raised his chin real quick. He has smooth golden eyebrows that turn glistening and downy at his temples. He has soft stubble on his chin. He took a few cigarettes and handed back the pack, so I pocketed it. Lucky for me he had a light because I sure didn't. I looked to the ground for an instant, it seemed, and he was gone. But I knew he would be back.

The staircase to the hospital basement is wide white linoleum and the basement hardly seems to be one, even though it is underground. It is not dank or scary at all. It is wide open, with a lobby surrounded by shops like a small barber and a little PX that sells essentials for the soldiers—toothpaste, sodas, snacks. The vending machines are on the opposite wall from the PX, near the phone booths and elevator. When my feet hit the bottom stair the place is deserted, but then it is like some absurd drama and it fills up with people so fast. A couple of guys come out of the barber, the elevator door opens and releases a bunch of people, a crowd seems to come from nowhere, and there is no way I am approaching the cigarettes now. So instead I veer off toward the PX so that I can keep moving and look natural, like I know what I am doing. Maybe I can browse in the PX and not attract attention.

I wander through the shampoos and then through the section with stuff to clean your car. Boring. Then I go down the candy aisle, looking at all the American candies that I miss somewhat for eating so many goomeys. When they are all in one place, all the candies, it is amazing there are so many choices. I remember some I used to love, like Baby Ruth. And Butterfingers. Then the box of Bazooka Joe bubblegum, my favorite bubblegum, bar none.

I run my fingers over the candies and dig my hand into the abundance of Bazooka Joe, but I come up empty-handed. I have no appetite for any of them. It is a strange and sad sensation—no appetite for candy? I need only the cigarettes so that I can please Angel.

I glance out the door of the PX, and the lobby area is clearing. Maybe this is the moment to stride across the open space and nab my cigs. The coast still looks clear, like a wave has pulled back from the shore and all is quiet. I feel as if I am held in that candy aisle, though, like I cannot leave, like I should want to buy something, some kind of American candy—but what do I want?

And then the weirdest thing happens, or rather I do the weirdest thing. I have no idea why I do this and it is almost as if it is not me, but I do it with my left hand, like the left side of my body takes over and the dominant right side has no control. With my left hand I reach for a box of Good & Plenty and pocket it. I don't even like Good & Plenty. In fact, I intensely dislike licorice, and that is what Good & Plenty is, licorice with pink and white fancy coating, but that cannot hide that it is licorice, which I despise. My left hand grabs a box and quietly, without the candy even rattling inside, stuffs it into my left coat pocket, and my legs take me past the cash register man and out the door, across the deserted lobby, and toward the cigarette vending machine.

From the corner of my eye I see a man ascending the stairs, his back to me, but no other people. No one is watching. The machine looms closer, and then I hear the elevator ding, which tells me shortly it will disgorge passengers and I no longer will be alone on my quest for cigarettes. I hurry, reaching into my right cords pocket, feeling around the crushed pack for the coins I brought for this purchase.

"Excuse me, young lady," I hear. It takes a second for the male voice to register as being addressed to me. I stop and turn, years of learned good behavior telling me to listen to the adult voice even though the cigarettes beckon. It is an MP in uniform, army fatigues tucked into hardcore black lace-up boots, a holster around his waist, billy club, gun. I look up into his dark eyes. He is not much older than some of the kids at the AYA on Saturday nights. His skin is light, but he has no hair or beard for me to know its color.

"Pardon me," he says, "but would you please return to the PX with me?"

"Oh. Well, why?" I say. "I've already been in there. I have to go home."

My heart pounds, and it feels like it has moved up into my throat. My ears buzz, so I take some really deep breaths and keep eye contact with the MP. He doesn't look mad; he is businesslike. He caught me, I know, but what comes next? The lobby fills again with people coming and going, and I know that a girl standing with an MP is a curious sight. I feel as if on display, like everyone is watching even as they swirl about me.

"Miss, I believe you have in your possession a candy that you didn't pay for," the MP says, holding his ground. I almost laugh at how formal he speaks. Plus I am so nervous, and sometimes laughing is just what happens to me. He persists: "I'll need to follow procedures, which begins with taking you back to the PX to return the stolen goods."

I cannot argue even if I want to. I have no words. I refuse to take a step away from where I stand. My right hand is still deep in my right pocket, clutching the coins meant for the cigs. My left hand, the criminal, hangs free at my side. I feel my heart crawl back from my throat into my chest.

"It was a mistake," I say finally, quietly, looking down at his big black boots.

"What, miss?" he says. I raise my eyes to his.

"It was a mistake," I say, louder. "I don't know why I took them.

Here"—*my left hand digs into the pocket and pulls out the box of Good & Plenty*—"I don't even like them. I hate them."

The MP does not say anything.

"Here. You want them?" *I ask, holding out the box.* "Take them. They're free."

What am I thinking?

"Alright, miss," *the cop says. He is trying to rally authoritativeness, but it doesn't seem natural for him. Just as I try to formulate a better argument, he says,* "I'm sorry, but I have to detain you and call your parents. We'll need to go back to the PX."

No, not my parents. Why do we have to bring them into this? This is not going well.

"Come on this way, miss," *the MP says, and I reluctantly follow. I stand outside the door to the PX while the MP goes in to tattle on me to the cashier, I suppose, and I resist the urge to run. I could toss the candy in a corner and just fly. Before I have a moment to act, the cashier, an older balding man wearing thick black-rimmed glasses smeared with body oils and flecked with dandruff, comes out to berate me.*

"Stole candy, did you?" *he says, smirking. Does he enjoy this? He yanks up his pants higher on his big belly.* "That all you got?"

"Yes..."

"Is that all she got?" *he says, turning to the MP.* "Not uncommon for 'em to take more. Them that do'll lie too."

"That's all she has, sir," *says the MP.*

"Did you check? One who takes some'll take a lot."

The old guy stares at me, as if to make double sure of my dishonesty. With him standing right there, overseeing it all, the MP pats down my pockets, the ones of my purple maxi and also of my cords. I know he feels the crushed cigarette pack, and he ignores it. He looks at me as he straightens up and steps back. I see a fleeting kindness in those dark eyes, and then he gets all businesslike again.

"That's all she's got," *he says. I hand over the disgusting licorice candy to the cashier.*

"I don't want to see you in here anymore, girl," *says the old man.* "Don't even think about coming in here 'til your daddy's shipped out."

I struggle with that logic. Then he addresses the MP.

"You'll finish up with her, won't you? You call and tell her daddy too."

"Yessir," *says the MP, and he takes my elbow and leads me out of view of the PX. We stop at the foot of the stairs leading out of the basement.*

"I wouldn't come around here anymore," he says, and he glances over his shoulder. He has become my big brother, like a nice big brother who is an MP and wants to take care of me. "You don't need to be down here. This place is for soldiers and medical personnel. Go home."

I do not wait. I do not even say thank you. I spin on my heels and gallop the stairs, up to the main floor lobby, where I run toward the back doors with my purple coat flying behind me, into the arms of the woods.

Little Oktoberfest, 1970

IT WAS SATURDAY night, and I finally convinced myself to go to Little Oktoberfest at least once this season. It would not be around much longer and had overstayed its usual schedule, maybe because business was so good. November had dawned, though, and Oktoberfest seemed out of place. In a way that helped me make the decision to go and see Kirsch. I too felt out of place, out of time. I felt so alone.

My plans to go to Oktoberfest on this night did not faze my mom, because after all, it was a carnival for kids where I would be safe. I left the house, promising to be home by ten. I told her I was meeting some of my new friends there, but that was a lie. I was going alone to see Kirsch and Stefan for the first time in a year.

The trail through the woods seemed to stretch out before me so much longer than I remembered until I realized that I was not running like I used to. I was incapable of summoning the energy to run anyway. My body was changing. I felt heavier, as if my weight was catching up with my height. My chest hurt too. Not inside, not my lungs or my heart, but on the outside. My body was developing. Two small sensitive knots had sprouted on my chest, and I had to protect them with a forearm when I wrestled with the twins. Running only made them ache. I knew it meant that pretty soon I'd be in synch with the moon, with my own monthly cycle, just like Eliza already was.

I wished I had worn a jacket over my big wool sweater, but at least I thought to wear mittens and a cap. I pulled the wool over my ears and brows and let my long hair insulate my neck.

I did not enter the Oktoberfest midway at all but went around the perimeter of the encampment until I came up behind the round arena with the glittering lights. I wanted to see Kirsch first, and I called to her as I stepped up on the trailer ramp. She was way in the back of the trailer, as usual—I could see her in the dim glow of the overhead light bulb—and she lifted her head to me, ears pointed, so that her black eyes shined, edged with contrasting white lashes. I immediately wished I had brought her a carrot, so I yanked off my mitten and grabbed a handful of oats from the stash secured in barrels at the front of the trailer. She accepted them hungrily and looked for more while I rubbed her neck and finger-combed her mane and forelock.

I stood there for a while, basking in her warmth while she munched hay. Then I thought I heard footsteps and got a stab of panic in my chest. Kirsch felt my body stiffen and it seemed as if she held her breath too. From the corner of my eye, I saw a shadowy figure at the door of the trailer, but the light from the bulb made it hard to see into the night. I heard a slosh of water—Stefan's water bucket—and then there was silence. I relaxed again and leaned into Kirsch's shoulder, until I summoned the courage to go find him.

It seemed as if the night had gotten colder already as I picked my way along the fringe of the carnival. I knew Jurgen would be in the center of the arena, snapping his whip to scare the children. I could hear it. Stefan would be out here, working, hauling water, shoveling manure, beginning to pack for departure. I hoped I would find him in the semidarkness, but after a futile search I knew I would have to close in on the lights of the carnival and be seen.

The ticket booth came into view, and there he was, leaning on the counter and talking to Mutter. Neither one smiled. Stefan had grown—well, he was 16 by now. His shoulders looked bulkier, his legs too, and his hair was short. And when I called out his name, it was those same green eyes that riveted toward me in a flash, but just as quickly he turned away, with no smile, no nod of recognition.

"Stefan," I said again and then stepped out of the shadows so he could see me. I expected him to approach me, maybe even hug me. I wanted that, even though I had refused him a year ago. I thought he would let go of bad feelings by now. He loved me, he said. I figured that might still be true.

But he stood there and only turned his head to me but did not smile.

I took off my cap so that he could see my face, and I felt my legs taking me to him. Then I saw him glance toward Mutter and begin to walk toward me, meeting me halfway. He wore a gray knitted scarf around his neck, and its ends hung limply down his chest, which was exposed to the cold night air. His jacket was open and so was his shirt, at least a few buttons down, and I could see a chest that had muscled up over the year.

"Hi, Stefan," I said. His expression had not changed, had not softened into acknowledgement, recognition, fondness, none of it.

"Stefan, remember me?" I said, smiling. "Philippa?"

I couldn't believe I was reintroducing myself to him. Had a year of travels completely erased his memory of this American girl in Munich?

"Stefan is not here," he said.

What? *But here you are,* I thought, yet the words did not form on my lips. I felt my heart fall from my chest.

I blinked the cold from my eyes. "What? Stefan, what do you mean?"

He held firm, stood there, no smile. Then he looked down into the dirt.

"Stefan," I said, slowly. "Stefan?"

He looked up, off to the distance, not even meeting my eyes, and said, "Sorry." Then he turned and walked back to the booth, grabbed up his water bucket and shovel, and disappeared behind the bright lights of the arena. I stood paralyzed. He does not want to know me anymore.

I had no illusions of following him. It was over. I walked back to the post and, without telling my mom of my plans, caught the shuttle bus to the AYA. The forbidden AYA.

Wild Horses

BY THE TIME *I get off the bus, I feel less alone somehow, and when I turn around I notice Angel getting off the bus too. I didn't see him in the bus, but maybe he was in the back. I took a seat in the third row and I did not scan the faces. I have become more introverted. I do not search outside myself; I am trying to read what is inside. Eliza and I once ran through the big world, galloped through the woods, breathed deep and took it all in. I have no use for that now. I am processing everything I absorbed back then, so I am full and cannot take in any more. I like the AYA because it is dark and loud and anonymous. Nothing is expected of me that I cannot deliver. I can talk if I want, or not. I can blend into the wall or spin the bottle. Tonight is definitely a blend-in night.*

Angel catches my eye and lifts his chin in acknowledgment, so I stop and wait for him.

"Hey," he says.

"Hi," I answer.

We keep walking toward the building, but I slow my pace because I do not want to go inside with the crowds. I feel so good with Angel that I do not want to spoil it. Angel slows his pace and stays at my side.

"What's up, Flip?"

"I don't know. I'm just bored with this scene, I guess."

We walk closer, shoulder to shoulder, and I can feel him herd me off the sidewalk and onto the grass. We walk up to the building and then up against it, along the brick wall, brushing against the bushes that are planted there, until we hit the corner, and then he takes my

119

hand and pulls me around the corner. His hand is strong, and I am not afraid. I am open. I want to go where he takes me.

I can hear the band testing, testing, and Angel pulls me around the corner like I am a fish pulled from water, over the side of a boat, and I settle into his arms, my back against the bricks, and his lips cover mine. The world disappears. It is only Angel and I. His breath keeps me alive. An eternity passes. Angel presses me against the hard brick wall, but all I feel is his body against mine. My eyes are closed, but I see him from head to toe. I see his tousled blond hair and his square jaw, the width of his shoulders and his loose jeans. His hands keep me close, but he does not push hard. Wild horses cannot separate us now.

"DON'T YOU FEEL *like you're falling?" I say. "I have vertigo. It looks like the moon is moving, trying to escape."*

"I know," Angel says. "I like it."

After the kiss, we walked along the back wall of the AYA and came to another corner, breached it, and then pushed through the bushes and into a grassy clearing that sloped toward more woods. We sat down, and upon gazing up I was so taken by the big black sky that I laid back to face it. It took a moment, but I finally was able to see deep enough into the sky to detect stars. Now the moon outshines all and is intermittently obscured by thick and feathery bands of clouds that whip by like silk scarves. The moon is a waxing gibbous.

"Weird that it's so dizzying when we're on solid ground," I say. "And the moon's not going anywhere."

We are quiet then, and I weigh the idea of escape myself. Angel and I lie so close, but I have the feeling that he will not kiss me again. He suddenly seems so far away. Facing the vastness of the night sky, I feel as if I have nothing to lose. I certainly do not have Angel; I cannot lose him.

"You think a person can change a lot in just a year?" I say.

"What do you mean? In looks? Or in their personality?"

"Both," I say. "So much that you doubt you ever really knew them?"

"I guess some people could," he says. "Some people are different each morning when they get out of bed."

My chest rises and falls in the cold night air.

"I had a friend last year, and I just saw him again," I say. "He's acting like he doesn't know me. Isn't that weird?"

THE MOON CAN TELL

"Yeah. What the hell?"

I don't know, and my eyes well with tears. I take a deep breath to prevent the pool from spilling over. I keep my eyes wide and watch the moon swim in the sky.

"Let's split," Angel says suddenly. "Let's go to my house and have tea."

I blink, and we rise.

We run to the bus, barely catching it before it leaves for the post. Angel runs alongside. "Hey!" he calls out, pounding on the side. The bus driver is a good one. Some of them aren't, and they will see you in the big side rearview mirror and still keep on. This guy laughs. He has black skin and big white teeth. We make eye contact in the rearview. He pulls up and lets us on. "No monkey business," he says, showing those teeth. The bus is empty but for us, and we go straight to the back, to the long section of seats in the caboose. We sit at each end, our backs to the side windows and our legs extended toward one another along the length of smelly vinyl seat. We do not talk. I am still sulking about Stefan, caught up in the past, but why? Here I am with Angel now.

Angel lives in the post apartments, on the second floor. He pulls a pot from a lower cabinet, fills it with water, and sets it on the stove.

"Where's your mom?" I ask.

He takes two mugs from a shelf. "You know, I'm not sure," he says. "She's not around much."

I look at the tea choices while the water heats. Jasmine, oolong, green, Earl Grey, cranberry. I take jasmine, but I'm hesitant, nervous. It feels awkward to be in his apartment with no parents. Wrong somehow.

"Look," he says softly, sensing my concern. "It's okay, Philippa. We're just having tea."

We bring our steaming tea down the hall to his room, and Angel leaves the door open. We sit on his bed. I hold my mug close to my face so the steam rises into my nostrils and flutters around my lashes. Angel does the same. We lock eyes through the steam. How is it that at this moment no one else exists? Nothing matters but this very moment with Angel. It is a feeling that seems ridiculous to try to define or explain. It just is, and it is what I have always wanted without even knowing it. I want it to extend forever, for the tea never to cool and the steam always to rise, for my hands ever to be warm and our eyes never to unlock.

121

We do not talk but move close together, snuggling side by side, and slurp our tea. The slurpings coincide, which makes us laugh, and then Angel spills his tea on his hands, and he takes both our mugs and sets them on the floor, and then he pulls me close and kisses me. It is real quiet and real soft. There is no sense of beginning or end. I cannot hear anything. I feel so alive—no, that's not it. It is beyond that. Feeling alive is breathing and being and doing. This is way beyond that.

This kiss is perfect, yet it slowly evolves and becomes better. It becomes warmer and wetter. It becomes something I want even more with each passing moment. I feel greedy, but I relax into it because it has no end. I push my body closer to Angel's, and he somehow wriggles out of his jacket. His body is so warm and soothing. I am melting into his heat. He pulls off my sweater quickly, and our mouths part only for a moment. I open my eyes and there are his, and we stare, and the kiss keeps evolving.

Angel begins to lean, and he slowly lists toward the pillow and pulls me on top of him. He reaches up to smooth my hair and hold my face. The lengths of our bodies are aligned, just T-shirts and jeans between us, my chest and belly on his and our thighs woven. I squeeze one of his between mine. His hands are moving softly along my back, and I squeeze hard on this thigh, and we kiss so deep and wet and dark that I lose track of where I end and he begins. My hands move down his back and I pull him closer, squeezing my thighs, and then my body begins a slow sweet vibration, and Angel knows it, and he holds me tight to steady me and he keeps me close with his kiss and low murmurs, and we breathe together, finally releasing our lips to gulp oxygen along with long rhythmic droughts of each other's breath, and then we sleep.

Gabby Returns, 1970

THE GERMAN GIRL Gabby was coming for the weekend, and it was not of my doing. I hoped I wouldn't have to see her ever again, and now this. But my parents were doing hers a favor because they were going on a trip or something. It was really only one day, Saturday. I figured that out to calm myself. She would come late Friday night, and then her parents would pick her up Sunday morning.

My mom had not taken well to my insistence on no longer going to the Shores' over the weekends. Months had gone by. I wouldn't give her the only reason that she could understand, even though it seemed unlikely to her: that I was afraid of riding because of my fall during the show. But it wasn't that at all. I certainly couldn't tell her about Gabby's cigarettes, but anyway, it wasn't that either. And it wasn't really the tense atmosphere around the Shores' house, the way that emotions went from overly attentive to cold and distant with unnerving unpredictability.

I guess the reason I no longer wanted to go to the Shores' house was because it felt too set up and artificial. My parents were trying to foist a new friend on me, and Gabby and I just weren't going to bond like Eliza and I had, horses or not. I couldn't fake liking Gabby. The thought of another weekend in that strange-smelling house with that family left me feeling flat and helpless. But I couldn't describe that to my mom, because she would dismiss it. Even though she was a poet, with all those poetic thoughts and stuff, she wanted something more concrete from me.

"You enjoy the horses, don't you?" she asked. "These people have been so generous. Where else can you ride such well-trained horses?"

"I love Forella. I do," I said. "I just... It makes me nauseous to go."

"Well, Philippa, you'll get over that. You just have to get back in the saddle, as they say."

"No, Mom, I don't want to go. I don't like to drive there," I said, thinking about the gas fumes in the little cramped car and the clouds of cigarette smoke. "I don't like to drive with Mr. Shore."

As I said it, I knew how it sounded, although that was not my intention at all. My mom stiffened, her mouth closed. She had changed her mind in that moment, I knew.

"Philippa, are you okay?" she said. "Do you need to talk to me about something?"

"Oh, no. No, Mom. There's nothing wrong." We didn't need to discuss it further. She knew I was safe, but I knew I had seen Forella for the last time.

"Mom, what am I supposed to do with her?" I asked now. "I mean, does Gabby really have to come?"

"Philippa, seriously," she said. "That family took you in multiple times and let you ride their horses. Don't be so ungrateful."

That shut me up. Then she turned to me and said, "Take Gabby to the AYA dance."

"But I thought I'm not allowed to go there anymore."

"Yes, well, let's consider this a special occasion," she said. End of discussion.

It turned out better than I thought. The first part, that is. The Shores didn't even deliver Gabby until Saturday before lunch, so we hung around with the twins and didn't have to talk much. Then my mom made an early dinner and she did most of the talking with Gabby. When Gabby and I got off the army bus at the AYA, I had hardly said seven words to her. How mean I could be.

We went to the outdoor concession to get Cokes, and then I saw Chris. I guess she was going to sing, because she was dressed up, in a short skirt and a peasant blouse. I hoped she wouldn't see me, but she came over. I introduced her to Gabby, and Gabby reached out to shake her hand and smiled big and said, "Nice to meet you!" Chris smiled too. I smiled, and then we just stood there.

"Gabby and I ride horses together," I said, trying to ease the awkwardness. "Well, not recently, but before... We used to ride together."

"Okay...," said Chris, sidling away. "Hey, I better go. Michael's tuning up."

"She's singing?" asked Gabby, as she pulled a pack of cigarettes from her jacket. She was so casual about it. She even had a lighter.

"Want one?" she asked, when she saw me staring. Her tone was challenging. I knew she remembered what I had said in her bedroom that night after the horse show.

"Sure," I said, and I pulled one from the pack and lit up. We stood there smoking or, in my case, holding a cigarette, and I felt calm. I felt removed, and I watched the social scene around me with indifference. I figured we would listen to a song or two and then split.

And then here was Angel, standing in front of me just as I placed the cigarette to my lips. He reached out, grabbed it away, and threw it to the ground. Then he crushed it with his boot. "What are you doing?" he said in a low monotone, and he stalked off before I could answer. I followed, leaving Gabby behind.

"You have nerve!" I yelled to his back. "Kind of hypocritical, don't you think?"

Angel stopped and turned. "No, I don't think, Philippa. I don't smoke."

"Bullshit," I said. "I've given them to you."

"I take them from you to take them *from* you!" And then he disappeared into the crowd just as the band started up.

I could not stand this. I walked back to Gabby and told her we should go. She didn't say a word, just dropped her cigarette, set down her Coke, and followed me to the bus that would take us away from the AYA.

LATER, IN MY room, I opened the window so Gabby could smoke. I didn't have one myself. Smoking wasn't my thing, when it came right down to it. Maybe I liked the rebelliousness of it and the buzz I got sometimes, if I smoked it just right, without a coughing fit.

But it was just too much of a burden, a thing I had to get, to acquire. It cost money, and it was risky. And, after all, it didn't feed me or quench my thirst. It didn't make me feel happy or loved. It didn't make me feel safe. Kind of the opposite. It only caused problems. For me, at least. Gabby sat on the windowsill and blew her smoke out into the night. We barely spoke.

"We got rid of the horses, you know," she said, finally.

"No. Why?"

"Mutti told Vatti to move out, and so now we cannot afford them," she said.

"Oh, no. But you love them so much..."

"Ach, ja," Gabby said. "Yes, it's true, but it's okay. Maybe we'll get more horses later. I don't care now. Because of the divorce."

I could see that Gabby had more on her mind now, but I couldn't help believing that if she still had horses, maybe it wouldn't be such a hard road.

In the morning, only her father came to pick her up. I stayed in my room when she left. She trotted down the stairs, out the door, and into that smoky little car.

Stay Sleeping

FIRST I HEAR their voices, muffled but happy, from their bedroom next door. I am in my bed, *I think.* Should I open my eyes? *My head doesn't hurt anymore, and I feel cool. Then I peek through my lashes and see my room, dim on this overcast morning. I roll over onto my side to relieve my back. It is stiff from lying there so long. And then I fall back to sleep.*

I WAKE UP again, and two yellow goomey snakes are on my pillow. Their scent conjures memories, so I twist to the other side, tighten into a ball, and will myself back to sleep.

MY MOM BRINGS soup, and I manage three spoonfuls. I don't talk. Later my dad looks in. He sits by me, holds my hand in his big warm hand, and it is nighttime again. I sleep a restful sleep.

Vergessen Sie Nicht, 1970

"HEY, WAKE UP," I said. Angel's eyes opened.

I needed to tell him that I had seen the goomey lady at the cemetery. I hadn't seen her in so long because the store had closed. But there she was, and then she was gone, so I turned from the cemetery and walked toward Angel's place. But then I caught a glimpse of her, off to the left, in front of a grave. I slowed and turned in her direction, and then I was at her side.

We stood for long moments at a new grave. It didn't have a headstone yet. Then the goomey lady bent down to pick up Spurlos. He wriggled in her arms and licked his chops. I had never seen his little face so close. He had bulging eyes with spiky brown brows. I had to touch him. His fur was short and wiry, and he closed his eyes when I stroked him. The goomey lady said nothing, and the cemetery was quiet.

Her gloved hand came up, and she was holding a photograph of a girl, around 10 years old.

"Meine Tochter," she said. The girl was her daughter.

"Sie ist fröhlich," I said. She did look happy, and she had dark hair, like her mother's. The picture wasn't posed, like in a school photo. It was more of a snapshot, and the girl was running toward the camera.

The goomey lady didn't say anything else. I didn't know what to say myself. And then she turned, set Spurlos down, and let him lead her away, along the gravel path that led out of the cemetery.

Please be home please be home, I thought, as I bounded up the stairs to Angel's place. The door to his apartment was unlocked and cracked, so I pushed it open and walked down the hall to his room.

Now he leaned up on his elbow. "What's up?"

"Come with me back to the cemetery," I said, breathing hard.

Showing no emotion, he rolled out of bed and pulled on a T-shirt. He was already wearing jeans. He ran fingers through his hair as he walked toward the kitchen for a Coke. I loved him for his willingness, for his forgiveness considering that I cussed him about the cigarettes. And then we were out the door, holding hands.

"So this is that place you told me about? I mean, with the baby graves?"

"Yeah. I was just there. We need tools. From my house."

"What are we burying?"

I wasn't in the mood for jokes, so I broke free from his hand and sped up. I felt a force inside of me, a tightening in my chest, and I needed to finish this thing.

In my carport was a tool locker with the lawn mower and yard tools and other random stuff. I yanked open the door so it banged on its hinges, and then when I pulled out the rake, along came a broom and a shovel too, and they all clattered into a pile in front of me.

"Hey, cool it," Angel said. "What's up?"

My voice came out hard: "I went to the cemetery. I was looking for something. I don't know what. But I saw her. I saw the goomey lady."

"From the store?"

"It was weird. She looked bad."

"What do you mean, bad?"

"Like she was crying. She had that dog too. It freaked me out."

"Why?"

I shrugged and realized I didn't want to talk about it anymore. I didn't want to tell Angel about the photo. Nothing against him, but I needed more time to think about it.

"Come on," I said. "Let's get going."

Then we both bent down to pick up the tools and bumped heads. I mean, *bang*. So we were both standing there rubbing our heads when my mom came around the corner.

"There you are," she said. "Hi, Angel. Philippa, we need to talk." Then: "What are you digging around in there for?"

"Nothing," I said, bending over again to gather the tools and drown out my lie. "What's to talk about?" I realized that was the old me, talking smack, having attitude. I knew better. I didn't have any reason to be resentful of my mom. When I got better after being so sick, my parents and I talked. We covered a lot of ground about love and trust and respect. My mom said she didn't want to fight with me as I grew up. She told me she wanted to be on my side. I felt a lot of weight fall from my shoulders when she said that.

Now she didn't react to my tone. "Come in for a minute, okay?" she said. "Let's sit down together for a minute."

Angel and I followed her inside and sat beside each other on the couch, but my mom didn't sit down. She paced, slowly, choosing her words, and the slowness with which she delivered the news made me dizzy and sick. It was all happening. All the worst stuff. I felt Angel's arm around my shoulders then, and he drew me closer.

"... three days ago. So they are watching her closely," my mom was saying, and my ears were buzzing. "It was alcohol poisoning, they said. I... oh, Philippa, are you okay?"

My head spun, so I took deep breaths.

"When was this?" I said.

"Dr. Romin just called," my mom said. "I wanted you to know right away. I mean, Eliza's all right. But, Phil, did you know she was drinking alcohol?"

The bottle, I thought. "What? No."

Angel took my hand.

I didn't tell her that I drank from the bottle that time in Sebastian's Woods. It had knocked me out. I wondered why I hadn't pegged it as alcohol rather than medicine. I realized that sometimes I kept secrets from myself.

My mom paced quietly, and I felt like I was holding my breath. I breathed. "So, Philippa, the thing is that Eliza's mom died last week. I'm so sorry. I just found that out too."

That's when I started crying. It started behind my nose, a squeezing feeling, and then my eyes stung and the tears made me sniffle and cough so that I began to really sob, with my face in my hands. I felt so terrible for Eliza.

"And so Eliza took it hard," my mom continued. "And then she disappeared for most of a night, and that's when this happened. But she had come home, Philly. She was alone, but she was home."

I finally saw it all from Eliza's point of view. I had been so busy feeling sorry for me, for poor little Philippa, left alone in Germany with no best friend. But what about Eliza? She had to move to a new place. She had to go somewhere that she knew no one. She had to leave me.

And then the worst thing that could happen finally did, and her mother was gone. Her mother had died. I could hardly breathe for crying.

Angel had his arms around me. My mom knelt down in front of me.

"Philippa, listen," she said. She took my hands in hers. "Your friend is going to be okay. This is terrible, I know. But, honey, take it easy. Just breathe."

She placed a pillow behind me and gently settled me back on the couch. Angel sat with me while she went to the kitchen for water.

We didn't say anything.

Then my chest relaxed and my breathing slowed as I became aware of something, that Eliza was alive. I realized that, somehow, I had thought she died, after she left Germany. I mean, not on a conscious level. But my loss had been so acute that it was like having her die.

"It's not your fault," Angel was saying.

"Yeah, I know," I said. *But she must be so miserable,* I thought. I felt bad for Eliza at the same time as I felt relieved for myself. I felt like I was rising from a deep hole, like I was coming back to life.

My mom reappeared and set glasses of water on the table. "Dr. Romin asked me to check in with him after I told you. He wants to be sure you're okay. I want to tell him not to worry about you. Can I tell him that, baby?"

"Yes. Maybe I can talk to her?"

"Let's wait. Let's let things settle down," she said. "Give it a few days, okay?"

ANGEL AND I grabbed the rake and broom and went to the baby graveyard. The sequestered grounds of the cul-de-sac were as untidy as they had been the day I went sprawling to the ground after running to hide from Eliza. Just as I remembered it, there were seven headstones—and the well.

The first thing I did was rake away all the leaves, down to the dirt ground, revealing each engraved headstone. Angel swept away the dirt from the surface of the stones so that we could easily read the engravings. All the children were under four years old.

Just that little effort improved the plot immensely, but it needed color, so we walked among the other graves, taking a flower or two from any that were generously endowed, and then I placed the flowers across the children's headstones.

As a final touch, I stuck a feather whip in the soft ground beside each headstone so that each grave had a little feather sentinel. Each grave had angel wings of its own.

Then I turned to the well. I felt in my pocket for a spare pfennig while I tried to come up with a wish, but instead my fingers touched the silver-white lasso of Kirsch's mane. The coarse and fragrant gathering of silver. And I left it in the bottom of my pocket.

As I leaned over the edge of the well, I was surprised to see the full moon staring up at me from way deep below.

But, no. It wasn't the moon. It was a circular cutout of the blue sky. Because then, there appeared my face, looking back up at me, reflected in rainwater at the bottom of the well.

Made in the USA
Columbia, SC
08 April 2018